AWAY FROM KEYBOARD COLLECTION

SIGHTS

CPATRICIA D, EDDY

Interior Formatting: The Novel Fixer

Editing: Jayne Frost

Proofreading: Darcy Jayne

We're all stories in the end. Make it a good one, eh?
 -Doctor Who

PROLOGUE

Royce

SOMEONE SHUT off the damn microwave.

Or did I leave my car door open? My brain feels like goddamn swiss cheese, and I don't know where the hell I am. All I know is that fucking beeping is going to drive me insane.

And what's with the smell? Disinfectant burns my nose, my throat's on fire, and I've got a headache that won't quit.

Turn on the lights. Why can't I see?

Assess. Plan. Then act.

Training takes over, and I force my heart rate to slow. The beeping slows too.

I'm on my back. My eyes are closed. Conversations provide steady low-level background noise, but I can't make out any of the words—they're too far away.

After a deep breath, panic sets in. Rough sheets stretch across my naked body. I try to move, but my limbs are heavy, unresponsive, and even my eyelids won't obey. Pressure tightens around my right arm above the elbow to the point of pain, then releases with a hiss.

Hospital. Tumor. Surgery.

My fragmented memories start to coalesce. In the misty recesses of my consciousness, I hear my surgeon's voice. *"We won't know anything for sure until we go in there."*

My hand trembles as I try to make a fist, and a deep ache draws a grunt from my raw throat.

"Royce?" Warm fingers brush my arm, and I force my eyes open.

Cam's worried face moves in and out of focus. I need to ask her...something...but I don't remember what. I can't even manage to say her name. As the frustration rises, her brows furrow deeper.

"Relax, Rolls. You're safe. I know you're confused, but the doctor said that's normal. Don't try to talk or move yet, okay?" She laughs nervously. "Don't answer that, either."

I track her movements as she lifts a large cup from a tray and then presses a straw against my lips. "Just a couple of sips."

The water's lukewarm, but still feels like heaven, and when she sets the cup down again, I whisper a hoarse "thank you," but all that comes out is a vague "oo" sound. What the hell?

"No more talking," she chides. "Rest. I'll be here."

She holds my hand, and I can't stay awake any longer. I drift off to sleep, thankful I'm not alone.

When I next pull myself out of the darkness and turn my head, she's standing at the edge of a curtain, her back to me, talking to someone.

"They didn't give you any hassle over the gunshot wound?"

A deep voice chuckles. "Ryker sent me to his surgeon. Pretty sure a chunk of cash changed hands. I'm fine, angel.

No teaching for another few weeks, but I can supervise the kids."

"I wish I could see the first class."

"I'll tell you all about it tonight. I love you." The man leans in and kisses her, and I remember his face. West. Cam's boyfriend. She introduced us—I think. My head's still fuzzy.

She turns, and I meet her tired gaze.

"Royce." Shock and relief play over her features. Yet, underneath, her eyes are shadowed, her lips pale and pressed thin. "Your color's better."

"Tumor?" The word escapes as "oo-or" and now I know I'm fucked. It's nighttime. I went in at 7:00 a.m. The anesthetic should have worn off by now, yet I can barely move. "Aaam?"

"Shh." She rests her hands on my shoulders and locks her dark brown eyes on mine. "I know you're scared. They got all of the tumor. Totally benign. But while you were on the table, you had a stroke." Her eyes glisten as my breath catches in my throat. "You're going to be fine. Once the swelling goes down, the doc says you'll probably make a full recovery. They gave you this new drug...it's supposed to be a miracle worker."

The keening in my ears...is mine. Oh fuck. I can't talk, can't move, and she's staring at me like I'm about to die. Fuck, fuck, fuck. "Ow...aaa?" *How bad?*

Now her tears fall. "I can't understand you, Rolls. But I'm here. I'm not going anywhere." Cam pulls a chair close to my bed, takes my hand, and as she forces a smile, my tears spill over.

"'Morning, Royce." My doctor's way too chipper, and I glare at him. Or try to. I can't move my left side much at all, and I have no idea if that translates to my face as well. "So, good news first. No cancer, and we don't expect the tumor to regrow. Once we get you rehabbed, you should be in for a long and productive life."

"Aaa...eeen?" *And until then?*

"I'm sure the aphasia is frightening, but the worst should pass in a day or two. The clot affected your left side, which also controls a lot of your speech patterns. Can you make a fist with your left hand for me?" The doctor pulls back the blanket, and I watch my fingers twitch, but not curl. "Not bad for twenty-four hours post-stroke."

There's that word again. *Stroke.* Until this tumor, I was so healthy I hadn't had so much as a cold in five years. How the hell could I have had a stroke?

"If you have someone at home to help you with day-to-day stuff, we can get you out of here in a week assuming the swelling continues to go down and the drugs we gave you do their job busting up any lingering clots."

Cam steps forward. "His brother should show up on Friday." She meets my glare with a shrug. "I called him once you were out of surgery."

Helplessness leads to anger and more frustration. Then kick myself. She's been here for two solid days. She needs to go home. Spend time with her new guy and run Emerald City Security since I won't be doing so for the foreseeable future. Not when I can't even speak.

"Eee-haab?"

Doctor Grimes nods. "With where the stroke was located, you're probably going to have balance problems for a while. The tumor caused some scarring, and seizures are still a possibility. We're keeping you on the anti-seizure meds."

I want to nod, but my head hurts too much, so I make a vague "uh-huh" sound and close my eyes. Maybe if I sleep some more, when I wake up, I'll be able to talk. Or maybe I'll just slip away forever.

Inara

In my tiny garage, I disassemble my rifle on the large sheets of cardboard that cover the floor. Tools of the trade—bore brushes, cleaning patches, solvent, and a set of small wrenches and screwdrivers are spread out around me in precise order, and I pick up one after another, repeating a routine I've performed a thousand times—if not more.

Except this time, I'm crying as I work.

For almost two weeks, I've put this off, unable to face any memory of what happened in the jungle halfway across the world. But this rifle cost me too much money to ruin just because I can't shove my emotions back into the tiny, secure little box they usually live in. I don't run from danger. I don't give in to fear. That's never been an option.

As I thrust one of the bore brushes down the barrel, I see his face. The blood. Hear him call my name. His last, desperate breaths.

Gunshots echo in my ears. The AK47s the insurgents used, bullets ripping through metal, wood, flesh, and bone. West slumped against Ryker, begging us to tell Cam that he loved her.

The ride through the jungle, my hand pressed to West's side. The kid we'd rescued moaning in the front seat. Ryker's barked questions about Coop—and my terse responses that weren't answers so much as excuses.

The barrel slips out of my hands and clatters to the cardboard. Solvent splatters my shoes. I kick a stack of cleaning patches, then step on them and skid as I try to right the bottle before the caustic liquid soaks into the garage floor.

"Fuck."

I give up. As my ass hits the ground, I start to sob. But I can't even wipe my face—not with my hands covered with solvent. Instead, I prop my elbows on my knees, cross my arms, and rest my forehead against my wrists. Maybe if I let it all out—all the emotion I've been carrying around since we left that compound —I'll be able to move on.

His final scream rings in my ears. Two words. "Help me."

Help me.

Help me.

Help me.

Why did he go south rather than north? Why didn't I see him sooner? Why wasn't I fast enough?

The questions keep coming, and I'm scared I'll never have any answers.

My phone rings, and I raise my head. Ryker. I can't do it. Can't talk to him. Not yet. Maybe tomorrow. Or the next day. Definitely not today.

"Inara, I was shocked to see your name on the books. What's going on?" My shrink, an older former Special Forces officer, leans back in his chair as I sink onto the couch across from him.

"Something happened on my last mission, and I can't get it out of my head."

Dr. Jeffries knows better than to ask me for details. Instead, he raises a brow and waits for me to continue.

"We lost a man. One of ours." My voice doesn't waver, but I shove my hands under my thighs so I don't have to see them shake. "I had him—well, the soldier who killed him—in my sights, but I wasn't fast enough."

"Did you make a mistake?" The doc leans forward now, narrows his eyes, and pierces me with a frosty green stare.

"Yes...no..." I run a hand through my hair. "Maybe."

"It's not like you not to know." And bam. He's gone right to the root of the problem. "What does your CO say?"

"He says very little. Period." After a few moments of awkward silence, I blow out a breath. "The whole mission was FUBAR. They'd moved the target, our logistics specialist had to scrap the exfil plan an hour before go time, and Coop...he didn't follow orders."

Jeffries nods. "Then why are you carrying around the guilt?"

"Because..." Shoving to my feet, I stalk over to the doc's window. Lush, green trees surround his office, swaying gently in the breeze. As I stare at the branches, transfixed, I whisper, "I think I hesitated." The words tumble out in a rush as if I'm racing to release all the pent-up fear I've carried around for the past few weeks. "West was dying. Shot in the stomach. That much blood... he didn't have long. And Ry...he feels like he owes West his life. I'd never seen Ryker look scared before, but he did that day. And when I turned back to try to cover Coop, everything slowed down. Like I was moving through quicksand. I couldn't get my breathing under control."

A hard tug on a wavy lock of hair helps me focus. "If I can't put it away, turn off my emotions, disconnect, I can't do my job."

"Maybe it's time you found another one?"

The doc's voice takes on a harsh tone, and even though I know he's baiting me, I whirl around.

"I'm the best damn sharpshooter on the west coast. Hell, probably in the entire country. I'm not going to let one fucked-up mission take that away from me."

"Easy, Inara." Jeffries stands, and I force myself to unclench my fists, take a deep breath, and return to the couch. Once he's taken his seat again, he rests his elbows on his knees and meets my gaze. "What I'm about to say...right now, I'm not your doctor. I'm a fellow soldier. And a survivor of PTSD."

He lets his words sink in for a moment before he continues. "There is a very good reason there are only a handful of elite snipers in the world who've survived more than five years of civilian life. The dead take a toll on you. We're taught to compartmentalize, cut off our emotions, put them in a box and lock them away. But human beings aren't designed that way. The more emotions you shove into that box, the harder it is to keep closed."

Deep down, I know he's right. But I don't break. I hadn't cried since high school—until a few days ago. But now...Coop's death didn't just open the box. It fucking destroyed it.

"What are you feeling right now?"

The question hangs in the air between us, and I open and close my mouth twice before I have an answer for him.

"Out of control."

"Then you have two choices. Find a stronger lock for that box of yours...or let everything out and deal with the aftermath. But if you choose the latter, just know...you might never be able to fire a shot again."

1

Royce

TARA, the petite speech therapist I've seen every Thursday for the past three months, offers me her hand. "Keep up with your exercises, Royce. I mean it. Don't settle for this ninety percent bullshit. If you do, I'm going to hunt you down and sing *Pirates of Penzance* songs outside your bedroom window every night for a week."

I chuckle as her tiny fingers squeeze mine. "I want my life back." My words are a little slow, but Tara's never given up on me. Even at our first meeting when I spent a full five minutes cursing at her—which amused the hell out of her since I couldn't manage the "ck" sound at the time.

The light behind her eyes dims slightly. "Royce, you know the life you have now isn't going to be the one you lost on the operating table. You'll never be the same guy, hon. Doesn't mean you can't be better, though."

Better. I'd like to feel better. To feel something other than off balance, slow, broken.

Tara nudges my arm with her shoulder. "Hey. Earth to Royce.

I want to see you back here in a month, okay? We're going to have a little tongue twister contest."

"You'll sssstill beat me. But I'll do my bessst." Dammit. I still have some problems with the "st" sound. My clumsy fingers grasp the folder she hands me, and with a final nod, I head out to the waiting Lyft.

Three months after major brain surgery and a stroke and I have most of my mobility back. My doctor even gave me the all clear to go back to work. I know I'm a lucky son-of-a-bitch, but as the driver merges onto the freeway towards home, I don't feel that way.

Right about now, Cam's meeting with her latest client—one of the top coffee companies in the world. If she does as good of a job with them as she has with all of the other clients she's handled these past months, every Siren Coffee House in the city will be running our—her—security software by the end of the year.

I should be there. Coding. Negotiating. Leading the team of ten programmers at Emerald City Security. They'd welcome me back, too. Even Cam. She keeps telling me she hates that I'm not there. But from all accounts, she's kicking ass. I'd be a liability. When I'm under pressure or tired, I stumble over certain sounds and words, and my balance and fine motor skills won't ever be normal again.

As traffic grinds to a halt, I slam my fist down on my thigh.

"Your left side will probably always be a little weaker than the right. Most patients with your level of damage can't manage precision tasks like picking up an eyeglass screw or drawing perfectly straight lines."

Manny, my physical therapist—the last of a long string, as I went through them like water the first month—sat me down and gave me "the talk" when Cam's boyfriend, West, convinced him to work with me.

"You had a stroke, Royce. You didn't do anything to cause it, so stop

*blaming yourself and figure out how to live your life without the parts
of your brain that died on the operating table."*

At that point, I couldn't take two steps on my own. Now, I run
or walk most mornings, hit the weight room three afternoons a
week, and never miss a yoga class. In my free time—and I've got a
whole lot of it right now—I read every fucking thing I can about
miraculous recoveries and alternative therapies.

My phone rings, and Cam's name flashes on the
screen. "Hey."

"What're you doing tonight?" she asks.

I love her no-bullshit-no-pleasantries personality. Though I
think she does this so I won't have to talk more than the
minimum if I don't want to. "The usual."

"Spending the night in front of your computer, coding apps
like a madman, and avoiding the world, then. Not tonight. West's
place. Seven o'clock. Bring wine."

"Cam—"

"Gotta go. Siren's CEO is on his way. You. Wine. Seven."

The call ends, and I swear as traffic opens up and the driver
speeds towards my exit. Cam does this every couple of weeks.
While I admit, getting out of my house—and my head—is good
for me, I often end the nights missing my old life even more.

Despite my reservations, Cam and I spent so long not talking
that I can't refuse her. The one good thing about the tumor and
stroke? They forced me to shove down the guilt that kept me
away from my best friend for years.

All of the misery, all of the pain I held onto after the bombs?
They're still there. But I bury them now. I have to. Or I'll hurt her
even more than I did when my mistakes led to the explosions that
almost killed her back in Afghanistan.

There's nothing I wouldn't do to have that day back again.
Hell, if I'd seen the risks, listened to my team, she'd be whole,
and I would never have taken that chemical weapons disposal
post that probably led to the fucking tumor.

But, no one gets a do-over in this life.

Once the driver leaves me at my door, I drop the folder on my kitchen counter, then head out again. The liquor store's only a half a mile walk. Might as well pick up that bottle of wine now.

Precisely at 7:00 p.m., I knock on the bright red door of a small Craftsman on a quiet street in north Seattle. The headache brewing behind my eyes warns me this'll have to be an early night, and I dip my hand into my pocket, relieved to find the small container with my anti-seizure meds.

Cam throws open the door with a grin, but her smile falters when she meets my gaze. "Bad day?"

I shrug. "Just a day. They're all kinda the same right now." As I amble through the door, I give her a quick, one-arm hug. "Don't worry."

"As if I could stop." Her quiet words aren't meant for me, so I ignore the whisper and pang of guilt as I head to the kitchen to find West.

"Hey, man. How's it going?" West asks as he pulls a pan of lasagna from the oven. The retired SEAL looks completely out-of-place wearing a red apron in the cramped kitchen. Six-foot-two and a wall of solid, lean muscle, he belongs on the battlefield —or at his Krav Maga dojo—but no one wants Cam cooking. I can still taste the petrified chicken she tried to make me after I got out of the hospital. Pretty sure that one meal set me back a week.

"Same shit, different day." I kick myself as Cam limps into the kitchen, her cane a near-permanent fixture in her hand. After the bomb tore her to pieces, her injuries left her with chronic arthritis and joints that could give out any day.

I kick myself for the bout of self-pity. I still have seizures. I trip more than most people, slur my words when I'm tired, and sometimes I lose them completely. My fine motor control is shot to hell and probably always will be. But my mind is still sharp. I can code, follow baseball, carry on a conversation—even if it's sometimes a slow one. And I've got friends who care enough about me to invite me over for dinner to get me out of my damn condo. My ownership stake in Emerald City Security gives me enough residual income to weather the time off, and my brother, as annoying as the bastard can sometimes be, checks up on me every week.

I snag the corkscrew from the small wet bar in the dining room. "Sorry. I'm good. Really. A little tired. You?"

West doesn't answer as I concentrate so I can line up the corkscrew. You don't realize just how many things you do every day that require dexterity.

After three tries, I'm about to give up and shove the bottle at Cam, but then the screw catches properly, and I blow out a breath. The cork releases with a satisfying *pop*, and I hand West the bottle, not trusting myself to pour.

"Eh. Might have a job coming up." He glances back towards the hall as the doorbell rings and Cam shuffles off to answer it. "Do me a favor? Don't let her spend too much time alone while I'm gone?"

"You do *know* her, right?" I raise a brow. Cam's as independent as they come.

With a wry chuckle, he pours me a glass of wine, but when I take it, he holds my gaze, concern churning in his eyes. "Yeah. But she fell yesterday. The rain brought a bunch of oil on the sidewalk. She won't rest like she should, and after my last job... Fuck. She won't tell me how worried she is. Keeps saying she's fine. But I know better."

I nod. "I'll do my best."

A new, feminine voice from the hall draws my attention, and I forget my own name when one of the most gorgeous women I've ever seen breezes into the room after Cam.

"Royce, this is Inara Ruzgani," Cam says as she follows Inara over to the bar.

I hold out my hand, transfixed, and Inara's full lips curve into a smile. "A pleasure, Royce." A subtle accent lends a polished shine to her words—something between British and Middle Eastern, and I think I could listen to her all day. As she grasps my hand firmly, I'm mesmerized by her pale gray eyes and dark curls that tumble down over slim shoulders.

"How do you know Cam? Shit. I mean, it's good to meet you t-too." My cheeks feel like they're on fire. This is why I don't date. Nerves make my speech problems worse.

"I work with West. The...uh...side projects we sometimes take on? We've had dinner a couple of times. With Ryker, our boss." Her fingers slide from my grip, and I'm shocked to feel the loss of her touch.

"Oh. Of course." I turn, hoping her piercing gaze isn't because of my crappy way with words, and pick up the fourth glass of merlot. "Wine?"

"Thanks. I probably shouldn't—long drive tomorrow. But everyone tells me I should live dangerously once in a while. Off the battlefield, anyway." Her light laughter is infectious, and I hold up my glass.

"To living dangerously?"

We toast, and I'm drawn to her hands. No polish on her short nails, callouses on her palm. Tan lines from fingerless gloves.

West and Cam have conveniently disappeared, and from the strained look on Inara's face, she's noticed as well.

"Vacation?" I ask to distract her. "Tomorrow. Your drive."

Her eyes dim, but before I can pull my foot from my mouth—not that I know why I'm suddenly eating shoe leather—Cam returns from the kitchen with West a few steps behind, carrying the lasagna. "Let's eat," he says.

Inara skirts the edge of the table. As she passes West, she whispers something in his ear, and he slants a gaze at her. "Neither of you were going to do anything on your own," he mutters.

"You didn't," I hiss at Cam as she pulls out the chair next to me. "Tell me you didn't."

"Didn't what?" She bats her eyelashes innocently, but Cam's never been able to pull off that look, and I give her my best glare —the one I used as her CO—and she rolls her eyes. "Fine. We thought the two of you would get along. So sue us."

She's about to sink into her chair when she halts and pushes herself back up. "I forgot the Parmesan."

"I'll get it, angel," West says, but she follows him from the room anyway.

"Well, that's not suspicious," I say with an apologetic look at Inara. "I didn't know."

She relaxes a little, the corners of her mouth twitching slightly. "Fair to say neither of us would have shown up if we had?"

"Yep." I rub a hand over the side of my head. Though my hair mostly covers the scar now, I can still feel the ridges where the doctors cracked open my skull. *Dammit.* I never took my meds, and the back of my neck starts to tingle slightly, a sign that this evening could end up FUBAR in a heartbeat if I don't take action.

I rush to withdraw the plastic container from my pocket, and as I fumble for the lid, the whole thing hits the floor. "Fuck."

Inara's out of her seat before I register that the lid popped open and three pills rolled halfway across the dining room. We meet on our knees next to my chair, where she drops the escapees back into my palm. Our fingers touch, and as we rise, almost jumping back to our seats, she watches me. Her gaze never leaves mine as I take one of the pills and wash it down with a sip of wine.

"Everything all right?" she asks.

"Situation normal." Even more than six years after leaving the military, some of the old terms slip in, but if she works with West, there's no doubt she served.

"Good. Even if we didn't plan this...date...we're here, and that lasagna smells amazing. Might as well make the best of it."

Hiding her smile behind her glass as she takes another sip of wine, I wonder if there's any way she'll give me her number before the night's through.

Once Cam and West return, a single bowl of shaved Parmesan between them, we dive into the meal, and soon awkwardness turns to laughter and the comfort of friends and someone new sitting beside me. So what if this was a setup? At least I'm not spending one more night alone, only my laptop for company, focusing on the life I lost.

From the look in those alluring gray eyes, Inara feels the same, and I wonder. What did she lose? And will I get the chance to find out?

Inara

A gentle breeze ruffles my hair, but I don't move beyond slow, controlled breaths. Six hundred yards down range, a straw-filled dummy stands sentry. He's mocking me. I can hear him, though I never bothered to give him a mouth when I made him.

"You hesitated."

"He's dead because of you."

"Why weren't you faster?"

"Fuck you," I whisper as I focus on my heartbeat. Two fast. For years, I've trained to be able to control every part of my body. Breath. Heart rate. The tiny muscles in my fingers. Even how often I need to blink. My mind...well, usually that's the easiest. Turn off all emotion. Focus on the target. Do your job.

Nine years as a sharpshooter with the Rangers. Only the second woman ever certified, with more confirmed kills than I can count. Kidding. I know exactly how many I've killed. I've seen every single one of their faces. None of them ever haunted me. Until now.

One hundred and six.

My heart rate drops below fifty beats per minute, and I analyze the wind as a small dirt devil rises halfway between me and Mr. Strawman. Nine miles per hour, south-southwest, if I'm not mistaken.

"Shit." My watch tells me I hit the speed on the nose, but not the direction. Solidly southwest.

Up your game, babe. You're better than this.

I shift the barrel less than a millimeter. The smallest correction here is magnified a hundred times or more at distance. My rhythmic breathing becomes my mantra, my body relaxes into a pattern I've repeated thousands of times.

Until Coop's face flashes behind my eyelids on my final blink and the bullet sails wide as my finger jerks.

"Fuck!" My hand falls to the ground—only four inches as I'm stretched out on my stomach with rocks digging into my ribs—and I try to force the memory away. Three months. That's way too long to still be dealing with this shit. Except, with West's injuries, we've mostly sidelined ourselves. A couple of intel-only missions, low risk. No one in my sights. So that whole "if you fall off the horse, get right back on it again" thing isn't working so well for me.

Ignoring my training, even as I think I hear my old CO barking in my ear, I return my hand to the gun, despite my pounding heart, and fire again.

Mr. Strawman's hand jerks. Not a kill shot. Not even close.

Four more shots in rapid succession all land off target, the final one sailing into the dirt two feet behind him.

With a groan, I roll onto my back to stare up at the cloudless sky. My cheeks tingle in the breeze, and suddenly, I'm chilled. Unsurprising. I'm not in control. My heart rate is in the high eighties, and the fingers of my right hand tremble.

"You might never be able to fire a shot again."

Doc's words haunt me. I'm stronger than this.

Breathe. Believe. Act.

My personal mantra. The one I adopted in basic training. The one that got me through sniper training. My first kill. And all the ones after that. Now, the words feel hollow.

"Do better."

I turn my head, catching Ryker's hard stare. The man moves like a cat. With a dark cap pulled low over his bald head, a black sweater, black pants, and black boots, he stands out amid the green and brown grasses blowing in the wind. He used to be handsome—I heard he had a modeling offer before he joined the army. Close to seven feet tall and all muscle, after his time in Hell, nearly every inch of him is covered in scars or tats or both.

"You do better, asshole. And what the hell are you doing out here anyway? I could have shot you, you know."

"Not with that aim. Or whatever's going on in that head of yours. You didn't even hear my truck." Ryker drops to one knee, his face only a few inches from mine. "Caught a job. Exfil. Probably bloody. Get yourself back in the game and meet us at the warehouse tomorrow morning, oh-eight-hundred."

"We're a man down." I'm not proud of my petulant tone, but running an extraction with only three is suicide.

"Not anymore. I hired a new guy. Be there, Inara. And pack your shit away before you walk through the door. You didn't kill Coop. I gave the orders. He disobeyed them. If anyone's going to carry this burden, it's me. You saved West's life. And mine." His dark eyes narrow. "Roll over, get yourself under control, and take that mother-fucking scarecrow down."

"Yes, sir," I say to the air as Ryker strides towards his truck.

Orders I understand. Following my commanding officer's wishes, I do exactly as he says, and when the shot lands directly between Mr. Strawman's eyes, a single tear of relief tumbles down my cheek before I lock the emotions away and try again.

An eerie green glow paints the eastern sky as I pull my little coupe into a parking spot outside the warehouse Ryker calls home base. My phone's already turned off, my go-bag packed, and my freshly chopped hair hidden under a black cap. My braid was a liability anyway, and after our last mission, I found two centipede-like bugs trapped inside the tight twists. I'm not usually squeamish, but discovering you've been sleeping with bugs *in your hair* is enough to make anyone panic over the slightest itch for weeks afterward.

The music's blasting as I slip through the door, and in the corner, West climbs the salmon ladder, shirtless, sweat glistening on his cut lats. The man almost died three months ago, and he's pushed himself harder than anyone I've ever seen to come back. He signed on to fund some new program at his dojo, and I think he needs the cash.

"Showoff," I call up to him. "Save some of that energy for the job."

West jerks, his momentum forcing the metal bar up another rung. "Ryker called." After a grunt and another two rungs, he reaches for a rope hanging a foot in front of him, then lowers himself hand-over-hand to the ground. "Departure time is now 13:00. Something about fucked-up paperwork at Boeing Field grounding the plane. Got time for a little sparring...if you're up for it."

I shake my head as I fill my old blue mug with the caffeinated nectar of the gods. At least with West here first, I know the coffee's good. "Long drive last night. And I don't want to kick your ass and hear about it the whole way to wherever we're going next."

He arches a brow as he hugs a towel to his chest. With a jerk of his head towards the whiteboard next to the boxing ring, he reminds me that lately, he's won every single fight. Dammit. I used to be able to best everyone—even Ryker.

"You have an unfair advantage."

"Excuse me?"

"You're Mr. Krav Maga Iron Fist Daredevil. Teach me rather than show off one of these days."

West stares at me like I've grown a second head. "I'm going to forget you said that and go shower. If I were you, I'd shitcan that attitude before Ryker shows up."

Fuck. When one of the nicest guys you'll ever meet calls you out for being an asshole, you're in trouble. I lift the mug, inhaling the rich aroma, and then take a slow sip as West stalks towards the showers.

The coffee goes down easily, and some of the exhaustion pressing down on me fades with the first zing of caffeine. I sink onto the couch and cross my legs under me so I can rest my hands on my knees. If Ryker's stuck at the airport, I can take some meditation time, try and calm my scattered thoughts and my sharp tongue before I get myself in more trouble.

Deep, centering breaths war with the caffeine, but though the sight of Coop bleeding out flashes across the inside of my lids, I banish the gruesome scene and replace it with a tranquil waterfall in Costa Rica. My Zen space. I let the birdsong and the crashing water carry me away.

Breathe. Believe. Act. My mantra plays on a loop as I picture myself floating in the pond at the base of the falls, the cool water a perfect foil to my sun-warmed skin. *Breathe. Believe. Act.* My heartbeat slows, the jitters fade away, and a gentle smile curves my lips. *Breathe. Believe. Act.*

Grounded once more, I step out of the water, and with a final deep breath, open my eyes.

West sits in the armchair to my left. Droplets of water still cling to his dark brown hair, and his black t-shirt stretches over sculpted muscles. A coffee mug rests on his thigh, his fingers curved loosely around the handle. "Talk."

"I'm sorry." I reach for my mug, preparing to rise for a refill, but finding coffee nearly up to the rim, my cheeks heat and I nod my thanks. "My filter's broken. Along with a few other things. Ever since Colombia…"

"I didn't know him." West runs a hand through his damp hair. "But for a long time after that last mission with my team…every time I looked in the mirror, I saw what's in your eyes right now. Hell, the intel-gathering trip we had last month? I barely slept those three nights." Rubbing his side, he winces. "You ever been shot before?"

"No. I do the shooting. Did get stabbed once." I locked the pain away, the memories of the knife sliding deep into the fleshy part of my thigh, the blood, the pain, the panic as I realized the asshole had nicked my femoral artery. I won't go back there now.

He saves me the shame of having to avert my gaze by staring down at his boots. "I can still feel it. Scared the fuck out of me. I'm a goddamned SEAL. Our training teaches us how to ignore everything but the mission. No pain. No fear. No regrets. But you see your life flash before your eyes, and all of a sudden, putting it all away becomes a hell of a lot harder."

I nod, not trusting myself to speak. Only my shrink knows I watched Coop die.

West leans forward to give me a hard stare. "This is the life we chose. Every time we answer Ryker's call, there's a chance we won't come back. That danger used to be such a rush. Now...fuck. The whole way here, all I saw was Cam's face as I left. I'm damn good at my job. So are you. We can help people. And," he shakes his head, "if we don't do this, Ryker's just going to find someone else. I can't do that to him. I don't think you can either."

"No. He doesn't trust easily."

West snorts. "Understatement of the year." After a pause, he continues. "Inara, you didn't kill Coop. The People's Army did. You saved my life, we rescued the target and brought him home. Put it away. Or...tell us you can't and let us help you."

I don't have a good response—or any response. Thankfully, West doesn't expect one. He pushes to his feet to head back to the little kitchenette for a refill, pausing for a single beat to squeeze my shoulder.

One hundred and six enemies have died in my sights, and though I can recall each one, I don't dwell on those kills. But one choice, one brief moment of hesitation, and I don't know if I'll ever trust myself again.

2

Inara

THE RAMSHACKLE HUT outside a no-name town in Uzbekistan smells of stale coffee and rotting wood. West sits in the corner, his head braced against the join in the walls, knees drawn up, likely fast asleep.

In this job, you catch a few minutes of shuteye whenever you can, and I should join him, but I'm too keyed up.

Ryker left an hour ago to meet with our contact, and the new guy—Graham Something-or-other—patrols outside. I see his shadow pass by the loose slats next to the door every few minutes. Too soon to form a solid opinion on him yet, but he seems sharp and willing to take orders. Unlike Coop. I hate myself a little for the thought, but the man refused to listen to West. And Ryker hired West for his operational expertise. If Coop had followed orders...maybe he wouldn't have been on the south side of the compound in the first place. Then, I would have been able to see him without turning around—and maybe I could have saved him.

"I can hear you thinking." West's rough voice startles me out of my memories. "We've got—" he opens one eye and peers at his watch, "—three hours until go-time. Shouldn't you be meditating or something?"

"Or something." I pull a small mat from my bag and toss the piece of black foam down on the floor against the wall a few feet from West. With a sigh, I center myself, bring my hands to prayer in front of me, and then let my arms fall gracefully to my sides. Slowly rolling down, I feel each vertebra slide into place until I'm folded in half. Hands braced on either side of my head, I kick up into an inversion—a headstand—and engage my core to keep myself steady.

Yoga is supposed to be relaxing. Ha. Not the way I yoga. I treat it like a competitive sport half the time, but inversions do calm me. All that blood rushing to my head leaves my toes tingling, and I start my mental inventory. Arches, ankles, calves, knees, thighs, glutes... Each muscle group relaxes as I mentally traverse my entire body.

"Two minutes," West says. The man's one of the most observant examples of his gender I've ever seen. I forgot to set my stopwatch when I started my sun salutation, and he knows I never spend more than two minutes upside down unless the mission mandates it.

"Thanks." I let my left leg touch down, then my right, and roll up to standing.

"I let you off easy back at the shop. Now I'm worried." West meets my gaze, and his blue eyes reflect the harsh light of the single overhead bulb. "When it counts, are you going to be able to pull your shit together?"

"Yes." No hesitation, no denial, no hedging. "Once we get through this op, I'll be steady again."

"That's not good enough." He holds up his hand when I open my mouth to protest. "By all accounts, there are twelve hostiles between us and the target. If I can't count on you to keep me from getting shot—again—then I'm putting Ryker on sniper duty. And he's nowhere as good with a rifle as you are."

He's right, and I run a hand through my messy locks. "You can count on me," I say quietly. "I can put it away."

"Kinda hard to 'put it away' if you don't talk about it. I hoped you'd open up after we got back. But...all our training sessions and you never said a word. What happened? I was too busy trying not to die to ask." In a smooth move, West unfolds his body, then grabs the thermos off the rough-hewn table in the center of the room. He offers me the first sip, and the coffee settles my stomach.

Passing the life-giving nectar back to him, I start my stretching routine. "I couldn't see him. Coop." Clasping my hands behind my back, I open up my chest, then lean forward and let my arms hang over my head. My taut muscles let out a sigh of relief. "You and Ryker went after the target, and Coop headed for the guard tower—just like you told him to."

West nods, his eyes unfocusing as if he sees the jungle camp's layout in his mind. "Should have been two guys there with AKs."

"There were." Curling up, I reach for the ceiling as I lift to my toes. "I saw one of them go down, then heard a gunshot. Not Coop's M-80—one of the AKs. I tried to find the second guard in my sights, but he wasn't at his post. That's when Ryker came on comms—said the three of you were running hot."

"The kid fought us. Thought we were more of the general's men. Poor guy could barely stand, but he had a mouth on him." West shakes his head, then rubs the back of his neck. "One of the advantages of the SEALs. We could expose our navy patches, and the targets would trust us." He rubs his right arm, mimicking ripping off a piece of Velcro.

I nod, remembering how I used to do the same thing. "As I started taking out the guys swarming you, I heard one of the guerrillas shout 'Over here.'" Closing my eyes, I try not to find myself back in the jungle, try to keep my memories in that little box I can see but not hear, watch but not touch. "Once you went down, time sped up, y'know? Like I didn't have a second to take a steady breath, let alone draw down on someone. I was operating on instinct. See a guy, shoot a guy."

"Training takes over." He nods, then checks the pistol strapped to his thigh. Training, indeed.

"Ryker taped you up, tried to get you moving, and I had to take out the two hostiles on the hill above you. After that, I looked around for Coop, but he wasn't where I'd last seen him. I figured he'd headed for the exfil point. But..." My voice cracks, and I reach for the thermos again, hoping the coffee will steady me. "As I picked up my rifle, I heard something. This...desperate sound. I dropped back down, tried to sight in on this little hut opposite you and Ryker. That's when I saw him. He was pinned down but managed to shoot one of them in the head. Then, he tried to run for the corner of the building."

Stuck in the memories now, I turn when the Coop in my mind does. "He headed for the exfil point, and I scanned ahead to make sure no one was going to get in his way. That's when I saw the assholes on the hill above you, ready to mow you down. Three shots. Three kills. By the time I tried to find Coop again, they had a bead on him. And...I wasn't fast enough. There was so much blood. And his eyes." I shudder, remembering how the light had left them, the whites burned into my memory.

"The soldiers dragged his body away, laughing. That's when I hauled ass to get to you and Ryker."

"Fuck. I'm sorry. I didn't know." West shifts from foot to foot, like he can't decide if he wants to hug me, slap me on the back, or turn away. I don't blame him. He's been where I am—or so Ryker told me before he asked West to join the team.

He offers me the thermos again, all the camaraderie I can handle at the moment, but the simple gesture is enough. "Ryker doesn't know the last bit. About seeing Coop die. I'd like to keep it that way."

"Understood." I drain the thermos, and West swears under his breath. "I wish the fucker would hurry. We're out of coffee."

I laugh, then punch him in the arm. "He'd better. Or you're going to start going through withdrawals. What the fuck were you thinking only bringing enough coffee for one thermos?"

"That this was supposed to be a quick in-and-out?"

I chuckle. It's always supposed to be a quick in-and-out. Most of the time, it is. This op? Doubtful.

"I'm going to ask you one more time. And whatever you say, I'll believe you." West takes me by the shoulders, and his icy blue eyes bore into me. "Can you put it away for this mission?"

"Yes." I nod, taking a slow, deep breath. Telling him...helped. At least enough for me to get through the next few hours. After that...who knows?

The rumbling of an old Jeep shakes the thin walls of the hut no more than twenty minutes later, heralding our fearless leader's return.

Ryker strides into the hut with Graham at his heels. "All right. I paid off the local cops, and they're going to keep their patrols well away from the little village where our target's being held until daybreak. No promises after that. We've got fifteen hours to hike five miles, scout around, come up with a plan, and get the rich bastard out of there. Huddle up." With a sideways glance, he hands the op to West. "Do your thing, Sampson."

As West spreads a map out over the small table, I glance down at my hands, relieved they're finally steady.

Royce

An uneven piece of sidewalk catches my left foot as I rush towards Broadcast Coffee. Unable to steady myself, I crash into one of their outdoor tables—thank God the damn things are bolted to the concrete and it's too cold for anyone to sit outside today.

Yesterday brought a series of mini-seizures, and today, I feel like I'm made of glass. But West asked me to make sure Cam wasn't alone while he was "out of town," so I dragged my weary body out to meet her.

Concern tightens her lips when I walk—or stumble—inside. She doesn't get up from her seat, which means she's still hurting. "Okay there, Rolls?"

Once we got over the stupid bullshit that kept us—mostly me —from opening up, we reverted to our army days. The banter, ribbing, and stupid nicknames are all back. The closeness we shared...well, we're still working on that. Guilt is a powerful emotion, and every time I look at her, I have to remind myself that she doesn't blame me. Even if she should.

"Just had to show that sidewalk who's in charge, Pint." I scowl, enough of a response for her, and she digs in her bag for her wallet as I sink heavily into the chair.

"My treat. What's your poison?"

Fighting her for the bill never ends well, so I glance up at Broadcast's menu board. "Large electric shock."

Her brows arch. Sixteen ounces of coffee and two shots of espresso is hardcore caffeine, but I'm desperate for the jolt. I knead my temple with a knuckle, trying to soothe the ache I've had since yesterday morning. "Didn't sleep much last night," I say with a shrug. "One of those days."

She doesn't comment, but as she plants her cane and pushes to her feet, her free hand comes to rest on my arm for a quick squeeze. That's all the sympathy I can take, and I'm grateful when she heads for the counter.

She'll pepper me with questions about my health for the next hour if I don't distract her, so I pull out my iPad and launch the tracking app I've spent the past six weeks coding.

With no current responsibilities at Emerald City Security, I've returned to my first love. Apps. One thing you learn after a stroke? Priorities. I enjoyed being the boss. Building the company up from nothing. But by the time the tumor forced me to quit—or take a long leave of absence—I was a glorified paper pusher.

I'm not sure I can go back. I'm still technically the owner—on paper. Cam's running the place and doing a damn good job of it. She's a fucking awesome negotiator, and she's brought in four new contracts and three new developers since I left.

She returns empty handed, her voice taking on a flat tone. "The baristas here know me. I'm not trusted with coffee mugs. Jax will bring the drinks over when they're done."

"I can—"

"Don't." Her voice cracks, and she blinks hard before focusing on my iPad. "You got something to show me?"

Distraction. I get it. We're too damn similar sometimes. "Loc8-tion's viable." I smile, despite the headache and the tight band that's trying to crush my skull. "I've used the app for three days now. It works with my phone, my iPad, and my watch." I angle my wrist towards her, tap the tiny screen, and launch Loc8tion. "Since I'm not moving, the app knows I've reached some sort of dess-destina-tion." Sure enough, Broadcast's address flashes on the screen. "I can scroll through my location history for the past forty-eight hours."

"User-configurable? The time window?" Now her voice carries a hint of excitement.

"Yep. Up to four days. Any more and I need a better compres-sion algorithm for data sssstorage. But one day, maybe up to a week." I spin the watch crown and pick West's address from my history. "Tap the screen, and I can see the date and time I arrived and when I left. Press and hold and the app will show me how to get there."

The maps app pops up and tells me to head south on Roosevelt Way. I can't help the small smile that curves my lips—even though I can tell I'm a little lopsided today. "Now switch users on the iPad."

She does so, and her mouth forms a little *o*. "Locate Royce?"

"Yep. As long as I've got my phone or watch on me, the app can tell you where I am."

"This is great, Royce. Really." She taps the screen, and when the app tells her I'm ten feet away and spits out Broadcast's address, my watch buzzes.

Admin user is trying to locate you.

"I've already talked to the VA hospital administrator. She committed to tesssting it out when I'm ready, and if she likes the app, she'll recommend it to her TBI patients. Memory issues are big for anyone with a traumatic brain injury. I've got proposals out to a couple of the larger Alzheimer's organizations in the city as well." My chest swells with pride, and the ache in my temple lessens slightly.

"How can I help?" Cam slides my iPad across the table as the barista brings our drinks.

The frazzled young woman with an eyebrow piercing and full-sleeve tattoos smiles. "Sorry, hon. We're slammed. I brought you a couple of scones for the wait. Where's your other half? I haven't seen him in a couple of days."

Cam presses her lips together for a moment before she answers. "He's out of town on business."

"Well, tell him we got a new Columbian blend the other day that I think he'll love." With a quick wink, the barista nods at me, then heads back to the bar.

"Hey." I lean forward. Cam's gaze shifts to her hands clasped around her macchiato, and a muscle in her jaw ticks for a moment before she looks up in response. "You okay?"

"Fine." The word escapes with a hard edge, and she sighs. "Didn't sleep much myself last night. Or the night before that. Or the night before that..."

Of course. West is out doing his superhero thing. Last time he left her, he took a bullet to the stomach and almost died. "Have you heard from him?"

A raven curl tumbles free from her messy bun as she shakes her head. "No phones. Ryker insists they be totally off the grid." She glances down at her watch. "He should be back tomorrow—or really late tonight—if nothing went wrong."

Her cheeks pale, and as she takes a sip of her macchiato, the cup trembles slightly.

"He's a SEAL, Pint. He knows what he's doing. Plus, it's a three-man—err, person—team, right? Ryker and Inara are with him?" Saying her name brings up a mental image of Inara's smile and the light in her eyes as I asked for her phone number the other night.

"They've got a fourth now. A new guy to replace the one they lost on the last mission. I don't know him. Hell, West and Inara don't know him either. And I just...shit." Steamed milk sloshes over the rim of the cup as her hand spasms. The bombs left her with some pretty severe nerve damage that flares when she's stressed out.

I swipe a napkin over the mess without a word, letting her take a deep breath and steady herself.

"He needs to do this. Both to keep the Horizons program running at the dojo and to banish some of his demons. I just hate that I can't talk to him...that I might not know if he gets hurt again. Or worse." She drags her hand over her mouth as if she can't believe what she's saying.

"We're new, Royce. Four months? And I'm stupid in love with him. Hell, I've basically moved in with him. We spent Christmas with his family. And last week, I saw him pull my grandmother's ring out of my jewelry box and slide it halfway down his pinky finger. Like he was trying to figure out my size."

I chuckle, but that's obviously not the right response because Cam cuts me down with her glare. "You're upset because he loves you back? Because he might want to marry you?"

"Well, when you say it like that..." She crosses her arms. "I never wanted...this. A relationship. Everyone I've ever *depended on* in my life deserted me. I didn't want to need someone ever again as much as I need him."

Her words, tinged with an odd mix of sadness and frustration, resonate. "Yeah. You did." The vision in my left eye darkens. Shit. "Just a sssec." I fumble for my pill box, then wash two of my anti-seizure pills down with a swig of coffee.

"You were so fucking lonely, you worked yourself half to d-death. I don't care how many people you talked to on VetNet," I continue when she tries to make excuses. "Chatting on a message board isn't the same thing as having a partner. Someone who's always got your b-back. Wesssst ssssshowed..."

Fuck.

My tongue suddenly feels three sizes too big for my mouth, and I can't see anything out of my left eye.

"How bad?" Cam squeezes my forearm, and I close my eyes so my screwed-up depth perception doesn't make me any dizzier than I already am. I hold up two fingers—a signal that this isn't a major attack but won't let me speak either—and she digs her short nails into my skin. "Focus on the pressure and take deep breaths."

I hear her rummaging around in her bag, feel her grip shift on my arm. I wave my hand, trying to tell her she doesn't need to call 911. Pursing my lips—or trying to—I breathe in for a count of five, then breathe out for an eight count. By the fourth repetition, the room stops spinning, and by the sixth, I risk opening my eyes.

Cam watches me with her phone in her hand, thumb hovering over the screen.

"O-kaaay," I stammer, then nod. "Almost...over."

She raises a brow. "I'll believe you when you can give me a complete sentence."

After another minute, the pressure banding around my forehead releases with a hiss only I can hear. I extract my arm from under her death grip and then reach for my coffee. The caffeine burns a path down my throat, and the shock of the steaming liquid banishes the lingering tension in my shoulders.

"I'm good n-now." My words are still a little slow, and scalding my tongue probably didn't help matters, but I force a weak smile. "Nothing to worry about. Bad...cluster the past couple of...d-days. I spent so much time finalizing the app, I didn't take my meds regularly."

"And you're lecturing *me* about working myself to death?" Cam scoffs and leans back in her chair. "How frequent are the seizures? Don't lie to me."

I glare at her, but I'm not her commanding officer anymore, and she doesn't back down. "I have a bad patch every few weeks. Five or six in a day. My doctor says that's not abnormal."

"Are you driving?"

Now she's pushing too hard. My voice takes on a rough edge. "No. I took a Lyft here. And I get plenty of warning. Knew this could happen. Leave it alone, Cam. I'm *fine.*"

Her stare, along with the tense set of her shoulders, tells me she's not going to stop, and I relent. Fighting with her takes too much of my energy, and my body is already demanding rest.

"I'm never going to be...the way I was. The seizures are probably permanent. I'm always going to be prone to falls, and I have a blind spot," I gesture to my left, "here. But I can code, I can run most days, ride a stationary bike and lift weights and take care of myself, which is a hell of a lot better than letting that fucking tumor kill me."

She flinches, then stares into her macchiato. "Why didn't you tell me the seizures were that frequent?"

"Because I didn't want you to worry. You've got enough to deal with right now with ZoomWare and the new SpryLot contract. And West." Desperate to smooth things between us, I reach across the table and touch her arm. "You got me through those first two weeks when I could barely speak, couldn't walk, and thought I'd be that way forever. Hell, you and West practically moved in with me, and he was ssstill...recovering."

"My place was too small, and West's house wasn't wheelchair accessible." Her matter-of-fact tone would normally make me laugh, but memories of those dark days still leave me in a cold sweat some nights.

"I was so fucking depressed. You kept me from losing hope completely. I'll never be able to repay you for that."

Cam tucks a curl behind her ear. "You don't have to. But I thought we'd gotten past this whole keeping secrets from one another bullshit?"

Two can play at this game. "You didn't tell me how worried you were at dinner the other night." Cam deflates. I might lose my words inside my fucked-up head from time to time, but I can still make a damn good argument when I have to. "Look, we spent years not talking. We're used to dealing with shit on our own. Can we both admit we screwed up and move on?"

"Deal." She meets my gaze, and though worry dulls the golden streaks in her brown eyes, understanding wells there too.

I rise, a little slower than usual, testing my equilibrium, but my legs are steady. "I'm going to find a ride home, watch the 'Hawks, and be 'one' with my recliner. Want to come over?"

"I don't think a football game would do much for my stress levels today," she says. "And I want to be home—err, at West's—when he gets back."

"I can be 'one' with his recliner. You don't have to be alone." I lay my hand on her shoulder, but she bats it away.

"Alone is what I do best," she whispers, but quickly adds, "If he doesn't come home tonight, I'll call you."

Guilt raises a lump in my throat. I did this to her. Ran out on her when she needed me most. "Pint, I'm so sorry. I wish I could go back and...be a better man."

Cam pushes herself to standing and tries to hide her wince as she pulls me in for a fierce hug. "You're a good man, Royce. Stop apologizing," she says as she rests her head on my shoulder. "You came back."

I hold on for an extra moment. "So will he."

As I reach Broadcast's door and zip up my jacket, I pause for a quick glance back at Cam's table. She's staring at her phone, and her eyes shine when she brushes her fingers across the screen. She may not like needing someone, but she needs West like she needs oxygen. He damn well better come back safe.

3

Inara

SOMETIME BETWEEN TWO and five in the morning—I lose all track of time when we're on mission—we touch down at Boeing Field, pile into Ryker's van, and pass the trip back to the warehouse in silence. Graham, whose last name is Peck, sports a swollen shoulder from getting himself caught in the belay line as we made our escape from the compound, and West holds a cold pack to his jaw.

We're all bone weary, and the scent of the target's blood lingers in the small space. Poor guy was mostly dead when Ryker and West busted in, and he bled all over them. By the time they reached the exfil point, West's shirt was soaked with piss and blood and God-knows-what-else. He burned the t-shirt before we left, but without the luxury of a shower, that fucking stench lingers.

"You coming in?" I ask West when Ryker eases the van off the freeway. "I don't think Cam would appreciate you slipping into bed next to her smelling like a sewer."

He scowls. "She definitely wouldn't. I have to grab my stuff, but I'm going to her condo to clean up."

"She still hasn't sold the place? I thought the two of you..." At West's expression, I zip it. I hit a sore spot.

"New Guy," Ryker says as we trudge into the warehouse to retrieve our civvies, "you need to put in fifty hours on the climbing wall before I let you out there again."

Suitably chastised, Graham nods. "Give me two days, then I'll be here every morning at six and every day after work."

"You see the doc tomorrow. Get that shoulder looked at and let *him* tell you when you're ready. You're no good to me if you tear a rotator cuff because you pushed yourself too hard, too fast." Our fearless leader might be a son of a bitch, but he's not stupid. Or sadistic. Just in a perpetually bad mood.

"And you two," he says as he gestures towards me and West, side-by-side as we punch in the combos to our respective lockers. "Intel-only on Monday night after training. Be here at seven. All goes well, we'll be done by midnight."

"Yes, sir," we say in unison, though neither of us bothers to salute. Ryker would probably give us hell for it. He doesn't like being in charge, but he can't handle it any other way. Whatever happened to him at Hell Mountain—the infamous system of caves the Taliban used as an interrogation "facility" when we were enlisted—shaped him into one of the most lethal men I know, which is saying something for an Army Ranger sharp-shooter.

"Good mission," Ryker says quietly as I dig out my car keys and phone. "The second half of your pay will hit your accounts in the morning. See you back here for training in two days. You too, Peck. Just because you can't climb doesn't mean you can't run sprints."

"Yessir!" Graham salutes, and Ryker grumbles something unintelligible as he strides towards the showers. I don't know where the man lives, but more than once, I've wondered if he spends all of his time here.

My little white coupe sits on the far side of West's truck, and as I round his mint-condition old Ford, I swear.

"Just fucking great." My left front tire has a neat gash in the side, and my driver's window is shattered, glass littering the seat. A quick glance inside the car confirms that my radio's gone and a cluster of wires protrudes from under the dash.

West is sitting behind the wheel of the truck, the glow of his phone screen casting his face in an eerie light, and when I rap on the window, he leans over and rolls the damn thing down—manually. I haven't seen a crank window in years. "Something wrong—" His brows draw down as he takes in the shattered window.

Despite the late hour, he's still lightning fast as he hops out of the cab and comes to stand next to me. "You leave something inside?"

Seattle is famous for car prowls. Leave so much as a sweater in your backseat, and you're asking for trouble. "Hell no. Not even the registration. I lock all that shit up inside when we go on mission."

"Well, yours *is* the nicest car here." West gestures to Graham's beat-up old Smart Car and the team's boring, dented van. "Ryker keeps his bike inside."

"Listen, I hate to ask, but..."

"Hop in."

As we weave through the quiet Seattle streets, I glance over at the former SEAL next to me. "You text her yet?"

"No. I need to wait until I'm cleaned up."

"She really worried?"

He sighs. "Cam's not used to this. Loving me."

"I don't understand." Not that I've loved anyone before. Sniper training teaches you to turn off all emotion. Follow orders, do what needs to be done. The psychological exercises the army put me through were a hell of a lot harder than any physical training. Start to see targets as people, you're done for. Think about their families, kids...you might as well hang up your rifle.

He's quiet until we pass through the next traffic light. "She won't move in with me. We spend every night together at my place. But half of her stuff's still at the condo, and when I asked her when she was going to admit defeat and sell the place, she looked at me like I was about to take her puppy away."

"Did you ask her why?" Sometimes I'm too...direct...for my own good. This must be one of those times because West shoots me a look like I've just grown a second head.

"I can read her, Inara. You look at guys through a scope from a thousand yards away. That's your training. SEALs...we're taught to read an enemy's facial ticks, their body language. All the micro-expressions that tell you when someone's lying or afraid or cocky. Cam's terrified. I just don't know why. Given what happened the last time I tried to push her, I'm not about to try again."

"She's not going to break up with you." I may not be as adept at reading people as West, but I can tell Cam's head-over-heels for the guy. Even though I've only met her a couple of times. "How many texts did she send?"

"One a day. And I know her. She wouldn't let herself send any more. Even if she wanted to." Running a hand through his short-cropped hair, he comes away with a sticky patch that glistens in the street lights. "Fucking target got blood in my hair."

"This is why I stay high on the hill. Away from the fight." I hold out my arms, then find a piece of a leaf stuck to my bicep. "At least trees don't bleed."

As West turns down my street, he shoots me a cursory glance. "You solid?"

Am I? Our orders were to leave as many of the hostiles alive as possible. I took three shots. None fatal. Two shoulders. One leg. Each one landed precisely where I intended. But was that the difference? Despite Graham's ineptitude rappelling, the job went off without a hitch. The only life on the line was the target's. West never even drew his weapon. "I think so. Maybe I'll sleep the rest of the night without seeing Coop's face."

"You'd better get to it," he says as he eases the truck to a stop in front of my house. "Less than three hours until sunrise."

A few minutes before noon, after I pick up a crappy rental sedan, I meet the tow truck at the warehouse. Once I've verified ownership, I watch with my lower lip trapped under my teeth as my baby's loaded onto the tow's bed. The repair shop promises a quick estimate and turnaround, but I still feel bereft as my cute little coupe disappears from view. Not only did the asshole smash the window and destroy my tires, he also cut the brake line and pulled all of my spark plugs.

Chilled, an odd prickle racing down my spine, I duck back into the car and head to Shoreline Art Center.

Sun streams into the studio, casting a warm glow over the cold, dark canvas. Years ago, after my tenth confirmed kill, the army shrink warned me I needed to find an outlet. Some way to deal with the darkness taking a life creates inside you.

It doesn't matter that I'm only doing my job—that the men I kill would kill me and my unit in a heartbeat. Watching the light leave a man's eyes through my scope leaves a scar, every time.

Though I started out barely able to draw stick people or

sketch a lone tree in a desert of endless sand, I slowly learned. A couple of guys in my unit tutored me, and now...well, now my futile attempts to work out my anger and grief have shape and purpose. Color and shading.

Swirling winds rip through trees stripped of all their leaves. A dark vortex where the sun or moon might be steals the light from the forest, and blood-red rain slicks the rocks.

"Fuck. I can't show this to anyone. They'll think I'm insane." I drop my brush, turn, and stalk over to the window. One of the other art students who frequents the space shoots me an exasperated look. "Sorry," I mouth.

I shouldn't have come. Not as tired as I am. But the job always sends me here. Half the flight home, my fingers itched to pick up a brush. I scavenged a pen and a couple of napkins from the tiny Turkish airport before we took off so I could doodle while the guys slept.

Pulling my phone from my pocket, I scroll through the contacts until I find Royce's name. Something about his quiet humor drew me in, and I even tried sketching him on my last napkin, but all I managed to capture were his eyes. And the pain in them.

Would you be interested in grabbing a drink this week? I know this cool little spot in Pioneer Square.

I try not to watch the screen, even going so far as to shove the phone back into my pocket and start cleaning my brushes. But six of them clatter into the sink, spattering paint over the porcelain when he responds, and I jerk.

Tomorrow night?

Flames lick up my neck to my cheeks as I thumb out a reply.

How about six at Libations? I'm an early riser. I turn into a pumpkin by ten.

Great. That's attractive. Tell a guy you're no fun before you even go on your first date. But Royce's message flashes across my screen, and I swallow hard.

I like pumpkin.

Holy shit. No one's flirted with me in ages—at least no one I've wanted to flirt back with. I finish cleaning up and stow my canvases with a smile and a bit more spring in my step than I should have after only three hours sleep.

Maybe I am solid. Maybe...all the darkness I carry inside won't destroy me. Maybe tomorrow I'll have some honest-to-goodness *fun*.

Royce

The townhouse stairs feel ten feet tall after my workout, but I can't bring myself to use the ramp anymore. I grab the handrail and practically drag myself up to my living room. Why did I think it was such a great idea to up the weights today?

Because your muscle tone is shit.

I hate what I see in the mirror these days. Though I was never built like West, I lost a good thirty pounds between the tumor's side effects and the stroke. I'm still in damn good shape for a guy on the north side of forty, but I used to be able to bench two-fifty and today, I only managed four reps at one-seventy before my arms gave out.

As I chug my water bottle, my phone buzzes.

We're way past Thanksgiving. You won't find a lot of pumpkin around these days.

After an hour in the weight room, my fingers don't want to respond, so my reply takes me more than five full minutes with all the backspacing and autocorrect mistakes.

Then it's a good thing Cam and West tricked us into meeting. Everything go okay on your trip?

My phone rings as I bite into an apple, and I manage a muffled "hello."

"I really hate texting when I'm tired," Inara says. "We got in sometime between 'holy fuck it's late' last night and 'no sane person should be up yet' this morning."

"And you're awake why?" On my way to my bedroom, I stumble over my own feet and crash into the wall. "Shit."

"Royce? You okay?"

"Yeah, apparently I forgot how to walk. Again." Though I'm inwardly chuckling at my black humor, Inara makes some vaguely uncomfortable noises before I realize my gaffe. "You can laugh. I do."

"Um..." The tremulous uncertainty in her voice shocks me, and I panic.

"Oh fuck. West didn't tell you about my...ssstroke?"

Silence stretches over the line, and my heart sinks. No matter how many times the doctors and therapists tell me I'm not broken, I know I am. And who'd want to get involved with that?

"Listen," I say, desperate to make things easy on her, "I'm... something came up tomorrow. Another time, maybe."

"No, wait." She draws in a sharp breath. "That was incredibly rude of me." Her voice softens. "The first time Cam and West had me over for dinner, they told me Cam's boss had just had surgery. I figured appendicitis or rotator cuff or maybe a hernia."

"A hernia?" I chuckle. "Nope. Unlike most people, I know how to lift with my legs."

Inara's voice softens. "Royce, I'm sorry. If...whatever plans you just invented as an excuse to let me off the hook can be canceled, I'd still like to have drinks with you tomorrow."

I don't hear pity in her voice. Only regret. "I can reschedule that Netflix binge for another night."

"Are you sure? She's a cruel mistress. Always asking me if I'm still there. Judging me for parking my ass in one spot for three hours," Inara says, and we're almost steady again.

"Can you talk about the mission? Or is it a 'top-secret-I'd-have-to-kill-you' thing?"

Her laugh makes my heart race. "If I kill you, I'll be drinking alone tomorrow night. And that's no fun. We had to extract a businessman from a terrorist cell in Uzbekistan. Routine, except for our new recruit getting caught in his own belay line. The target's got a long recovery ahead of him, but he's alive, and his family only had to pay Hidden Agenda twenty thousand rather than send two million to the terrorists."

"No wonder Cam was worried." I strip off my shirt. "Uzbekistan's not an easy place to get in and out of."

"Cam didn't know where we were. Ryker's rules. No discussing the mission until it's over. No phones. No communication with family or friends. Too easy for a signal to get out. I hate it, but he's right to insist. What we do...one mistake, and we're all dead."

"How long have you worked for him?" Inara's voice does things to me I haven't felt in years. My shorts tent just listening to her, and I'd give any randy teenager a run for his money right now.

"Six years. I was part of the unit that rescued him from Hell. Or rather, the unit that escorted him back to base. Fucking tank broke himself out."

"Fuck. Really?" If you were deployed anytime in the past fifteen years, you know about Hell. I lost friends there. "How come that's not more widely known? ComSat should have shouted that from the heavens. The big, bad Hell Mountain vulnerable? That would have been huge news."

"The brass insisted. Way above my pay grade, but I think they wanted to try to lull the bastards into a false sense of security. Worked, too. Once he'd recovered enough to shoot straight, Ryker went back in and took 'em all down."

"He what?" I sputter on my water, spraying droplets down my chest. "Alone?"

That sexy chuckle floats over the line. "Definitely not. He brought West and his SEAL team. A whole contingent of Rangers. I wanted in on that mission so badly. But I'd taken a knife to the thigh getting Ryker back to Bagram, and my PT took longer than I wanted." Her voice lowers. "That's what you get for being stubborn and trying to do too much too soon."

As I try to sit up straighter, only to have my abs shake so much I fall back against the pillows, I sigh. "Know that feeling."

"I should go," she says, yawning. "I'm about to hit that pumpkin stage right now. But tomorrow? Six at Libations?"

"Wouldn't miss it."

Despite my exhaustion, I smile as I head for the shower. But doubts start to creep in as I sink into my recliner and boot up my laptop. She didn't know about the stroke. Stands to reason she doesn't know about the brain tumor either.

Seizures, stuttering, and aphasia don't make for fun first date conversations. And fuck. What if I lose my words in the middle of appetizers? Or trip and fall on the way into the bar?

Lines of code blur on the screen, and I can't shake the worry that tomorrow is either going to be the start of something—or the end of everything.

4

Inara

SONIA WAVES at me from the coffee cart as I slip through the doors of the Seattle's World Trade Center building. "Hey, love. How was your vacation?"

Plastering on a fake smile, I give her a quick, one-arm hug. "Not exactly a vacation. A friend needed a translator for an overseas business meeting. I did get to see Istanbul, though. Great food."

We all have cover stories. K&R isn't exactly...legal. The government frowns on vets sneaking into foreign countries, interfering where we don't belong, and sometimes—when it's unavoidable—killing people.

The best lies have a shade of truth to them. I usually try to pick a country or city a flight or two away from our destination and make something up. And hell, we did fly over Istanbul. Sometime in the middle of the night. While I was sketching Royce's eyes.

Conveniently, most of the world's large businesses need translators, which provides me ample cover. And my boss doesn't care where I do my job as long as it gets done.

"You're so lucky. Always getting to go to these exotic locations," she says, a hint of wistfulness to her tone. "Mr. Williams never sends me anywhere."

Sonia's a genius with contracts. A lawyer with the Port of Seattle, she works her ass off for a fraction of what she could make at one of the big law firms in the city.

"So go on your own. Live a little." She looks unsure. After a long sip of my quad-shot latte, I purse my lips. "Tell you what. Make sure your passport's up to date. Next time I have to go somewhere fun, fly out and meet me for a couple of days after I finish with the business shit. We'll have a little fun. Full warning, though. It'll likely be a last-minute sort of trip. I've got a friend who works for British Air. He can probably get you a deal on a ticket."

"Oh, Inara!" Sonia throws her arms around me, and I stumble back, nearly losing my coffee. "That would be awesome."

Laughing—since I saved the coffee—I pat her back. A little awkwardly. I don't have a lot of friends. Army buddies I keep in touch with over email and FaceTime. Yasmin, who bit me our first day of pre-school and was my best friend well through college, West, and Ryker. I suppose Cam's a friend now too—or will be since we've only had three meals together. But I like her.

My shrink keeps telling me I need to put myself out there more. Take risks. I laughed. Full-on belly laugh with tears rolling down my cheeks. I have one of the riskiest jobs in the world. But when you keep your emotions locked up tight, people notice. And they tend to pull away—or avoid getting close in the first place.

But Dr. Jeffries is right. I don't trust anyone with my heart. Or my safety. Sonia's sweet, and a girls' trip? I might be able to handle that. For a couple of days anyway.

"Wanna hit up Ivar's for dinner?" Sonia asks as she releases me and punches the elevator call button.

"Can't." My cheeks flame, and I'm lucky my mixed heritage—an Iranian mother and a British diplomat father—doesn't reveal my blush. "I'm...wiped, hon. Jet lag for a three-day trip is brutal. Raincheck? Maybe next week?"

I'm not ready to tell her about Royce. After my gaffe on the phone, I don't even know if we'll hit it off.

"You got it," Sonia says with only a hint of disappointment. "But maybe a movie, too?"

Sonia's all alone. Her mom lives in town, but their relationship is strained at best. Her ex-husband beat her, and though she's one of the strongest women I know, on rare days like this, I can see the vulnerability in her eyes. "Definitely. And come get me when you take a break this afternoon. We'll go grab a coffee. My treat."

The day crawls by. I love what I do. Speaking six languages—reading two others—makes for an interesting variety of projects, and I'm halfway through translating a legal brief from Russian to English for the local branch of the Red Cross when my phone buzzes.

I haven't been able to concentrate all day. The clock is mocking me. Pretty sure it's moving backwards.

My chuckle reverberates in my small, solitary office.

Only another four hours. Besides, anticipation makes everything taste better.

I can't believe I'm flirting like this.

Everything?

My fingers tremble as I type out my reply, hoping I don't scare him off before we even have a chance to find out where this is going. He's taken everything else I've thrown at him.

Everything.

The little dots under my message dance for so long, my screen goes dark and hold my breath.

Well, I hope you're hungry.

Oh no. I'm not scaring him off. Thank fuck.

Royce

I hope you're hungry? That's the best you could do?

Kicking myself for my very rusty sexting skills—the last time I dated regularly, this wasn't a thing—I head into the Capitol Hill Yoga Center.

After my phone call with Inara yesterday, I held myself to a very strict schedule. Work on Loc8tion, rest, work, rest, work, rest, plenty of water, no alcohol, a vegetarian dinner, and an early bedtime. Some days, control is all that gets me through.

Now, I'm standing outside my yoga class, hoping it'll center me.

I used to think yoga was for hippies who liked to pretend to exercise while getting in touch with their inner gods and goddesses, but during rehab, when I couldn't walk more than a few steps at a time, Manny dragged me to a beginner's class.

Thirty minutes later, sweat pouring down my face, panting, and feeling like a wet noodle, the son-of-a-bitch I nicknamed Sergeant Diabolical wheeled me out of there with a wide smile plastered across his "I told you so" face. I never made fun of yoga again.

Turns out, I even like the classes. They help my balance, and on my bad days, my regular instructor gives me seated modifications for all of the poses.

A little after four, I find myself trembling my way through a backbend with my mind on Inara. Bad idea. I crash to the ground with a muttered oof—no cursing in yoga—and lie there staring at the flickering candles for long enough that Basha, the instructor, rushes over to me.

"You okay?" He reaches for my arm to help me up, and when I'm seated, my cheeks flaming, I wave him away. "You haven't fallen in a month," he whispers.

"After class," I say. Basha nods and returns to the front of the room where he instructs us in malasanna, a balancing squat, and my muscles protest one of the few poses I've never mastered.

The rest of the class passes with a growing knot in my stomach. In the final pose, savasanna, where we're all supposed to thank our bodies for supporting us and meditate on the intention we set at the beginning of class, I'm going through code in my head, checking off all of the bugs I fixed last week. It's either that or obsess over my upcoming date. I'm so focused, I don't even notice the other students pick up their mats and walk out of the studio until Basha clears his throat.

"Royce?"

I open my eyes, staring at one of the soft lights overhead. The emptiness of the space surrounds me, and I sigh. "I guess it's after class."

"Need to talk?" Basha grabs a mop from a small closet and starts wiping down the floor as I roll up to sitting. "Most of your practice was flawless, so I assume your distractions are in your mind."

My legs shake as I get to my feet, and I drag my mat over to the door before half-collapsing onto one of the benches. "You could say that. I'm close to releasing that app I told you about. And..." I run a hand through my hair, stifling my wince as my fingers trail over my scar. "I have a date tonight."

Basha grins as he curves the mop in an arc and heads back in my direction. "Ah. So that's why you're off balance."

"Maybe. I haven't dated in...three years at least. Not since I started having seizures." The sweat drying on my skin sends a shudder through me, or...perhaps I've hit upon my real worry— what if something happens when I'm with Inara? "When she agreed to go out with me, she didn't know about the ssstroke."

As the yogi drops down onto the bench next to me, balancing the mop handle against his knee, he sighs. "No man—or woman —is perfect. Yoga teaches us this. You've seen me fall out of tree pose, and I've been teaching for ten years. That's why we call what we do 'practice.'"

He glances over at me, a serene smile on his face. His scraggly beard is gathered at his chin, a red band encircling the wiry black hair. "In life, we must accept everything. Happiness, grief, elation, guilt, joy, sorrow, chaos, and peace. We honor and embrace our emotions, and this is how we learn tolerance for others and for ourselves."

The Royce from three years ago probably would have snorted in disbelief and walked away from anyone spouting wisdom like Basha, but deep down, I know he's right.

"Go, enjoy, be present in the moment. If she cannot accept you for who you are, then she is not the right woman for you." He winks as he springs to his feet. "But even the wrong woman can be fun."

Fun. I've never been very good at fun. Between building up Emerald City and managing my health issues, I lost sight of fun. Even if we don't make it to a second date, a night out with an intelligent, witty, and gorgeous woman should be fun.

Half an hour later, standing in front of my bathroom mirror, doubt creeps back in.

Turning, I flex, satisfied that my six-pack has finally returned and my delts and pecs are on their way back from their stroke-induced vacation. My doctor would be proud, but I still see a sick, pathetic weakling in the mirror.

And tonight, I'll have to tell Inara about the stroke. What if she runs? Or...pity swims in her stormy gray eyes?

The one and only time I accepted Cam's invite to Emerald City's employee happy hour, I almost walked—or limped—out after ten minutes. No one knew what to say to me. Being a shit boss the six months before surgery didn't help matters, but between the looks of pity when I stumbled over my words and the overly solicitous offers to help me carry my beer back from the bar set me on edge.

Cam understood, at least. And hasn't pressured me to come since.

I didn't think I'd ever date again, but when I said goodnight to Inara after dinner at Cam's the other night, the heat in her gaze set me on fire, and I'm not sure I've stopped burning since. I woke up twice last night with her name on my lips. Why am I fanta-sizing about a woman I barely know?

Because you haven't dated since you learned about the tumor.

"I am the very model of a modern major general," I say with as much speed as I can muster. Those stupid speech exercises make me feel like a child, but they work, and I'll be damned if I'm going to trip over my words tonight.

"I can do this." I meet my own gaze in the mirror, the intensity in my eyes something I've missed the past few years. I just hope I can make it through the evening without a fuck-up.

Inara

As I head for Libations, a nervous flutter in my stomach, second thoughts kick in. First dates—and that's what this is, despite the dinner at West's the other night—are full of minefields. Family histories, college stories, hopes and dreams...and fears. Add in my shock and inability to find my words when Royce told me he'd had a stroke, and this could be a disaster.

At a stoplight, I scan the busy streets around me, drumming my fingers on the steering wheel. A shadow flits across my rearview mirror, and I flinch. The man in the dark hoodie jaywalking behind my car sets me on edge, and I tighten my grip until my knuckles turn white.

Pop, pop, pop.

Despite the cool air, sweat gathers at the base of my spine. *Breathe. Believe. Act.* I narrow my focus, peering through my scope. One target. One shot. A scream. *Help me!* Coop. All that blood. His eyes.

The car behind me honks, and I yelp as the sound drags me back to the present. I'm not on that roof in Colombia. The light's turned green, and I'm holding up traffic.

Making the left turn onto Yesler, I force myself to breathe. Across the street, a couple of teenagers set off fireworks for Chinese New Year. I hate fireworks.

Once I've parked, I massage my temples. *Put it away, Inara. Back in that box. You did your job.*

But...did I? Why don't I know? It's my fucking job to know. One second of hesitation, one breath, one heartbeat too many and a man died. Coop died.

Royce is waiting. I have to pull myself together. If I can't...then who am I?

5

Royce

A LIGHT DRIZZLE of rain coats the streets, and I turn my collar up as I stride towards Libations. *You can do this. She asked you out, remember?*

Except, she didn't know about the stroke. I can still hear her silence on the phone. Like a physical punch to the gut, reminding me how broken I am.

The fingers of my left hand tremble inside my jacket pocket. Sometimes, the muscles have a mind of their own, and I clench my fist, willing the tremor away.

Right on time, I pull open Libations' solid wood and brass door and step inside the warm glow. This early, the bar is quiet— only a handful of patrons seated on stools or chatting at small tables throughout the room. And Inara, waiting by the hostess stand, her dark hair now cropped into a messy—and sexy—bob.

"Hey," she says with a shy smile. I'm mesmerized by her eyes, a hint of kohl emphasizing the gray. Frozen, I don't know how to respond. Handshake? Kiss on the cheek? Awkwardness stretches between us until she leans in, her hand splaying against my back as she pulls me close for a hug. The scents of lilies and orange blossoms waft over me, and I drink her in as soft curls brush my cheek.

"This is new," I say as I let a silky lock slip through my fingers. "Looks great on you."

Inara smiles as she drops her gaze to her boots. "Thanks. Maybe sometime food isn't involved I'll tell you the story behind it."

The bartender gestures to the half-empty restaurant, his rolled-up sleeves exposing intricate tattoos. "Sit anywhere, folks. Happy Hour menus are on the tables."

"How about that corner table?" Inara whispers in my ear as she tucks her hand around my elbow. "Quiet. Out of the way."

I let her guide me, unsure if she's holding onto me because she's afraid I'll fall or because she *wants* to. At the last minute, I skirt around her to pull out her chair and help her off with her jacket. Her crimson blouse dips low at her back, exposing bronzed, smooth skin, and I skim my palms over her shoulders.

"Thanks." She glances up at me as I help scoot her chair in, and the heat in her gaze gives me a glimmer of hope.

Taking a seat before I get any more aroused, I pick up a menu, glad for the distraction. "Have you been here before? I think Cam's had a couple of team outings upstairs in their event space, but this is my first time."

"No. I...don't get out much." She runs her hands over the menu on the table, not meeting my gaze.

Why is she nervous? She's gorgeous. Witty—at least over text. Perfect skin, just a hint of an exotic accent, and her eyes sparkle when she smiles.

"That's hard to believe. I mean...w-work or was there someone special, or...?" *Fuck. Pull your foot out of your damn mouth, soldier.*

Before she can answer, a server with spiked blond and purple hair approaches. We're both martini fans, dirty, of course, and that leads to a chuckle, breaking up a bit of the tension.

Inara lifts her gaze, and uncertainty dims the light in her eyes. "No one special. Not for a long time. Between my job, Hidden Agenda, and training, I don't have a lot of free time for...'getting out.'"

"Training?" I grab onto the single word, hoping it'll be a safe topic. I'd rather not go into the whole "brain-tumor-stroke-couldn't-walk-or-talk-for-weeks" saga before drinks.

A single brow lifts, and she smiles. "Cam and West haven't complained about Ryker's insane training schedule?"

"No. To be fair, I haven't seen them much in the past few weeks."

With a slight quirk of her head, she searches my face. "I thought you and Cam were close?"

That's a whole can of worms I don't want to open all over this polished wood table. "We're...complicated. Lots of baggage between us until a few months ago, and we haven't unpacked it all yet. She's family. But until last fall, we hadn't really talked in years."

Guilt raises a lump in my throat, and as the server delivers our drinks, I take a moment to try to force those regrets down deep.

"Earth to Royce." Inara holds her drink aloft. When I mirror her movements, my cheeks flushing a bit, she says, "To trying a new bar with someone who likes their martinis as dirty as I do."

I couldn't respond if my life depended on it. My mouth's suddenly gone as dry as sand, and I touch my glass to hers before taking a healthy sip.

"So...what *do* you do with Hidden Agenda?"

"Sharpshooter."

Thank God I'd set my glass down. "Fuck. Seriously?"

Her eyes narrow. "Why 'seriously'? Because it's a *man's* job? I spent seven years with the Rangers—" The edge to her voice warns me I've crossed back into foot-in-mouth territory, and I rush to explain.

"Hell, no. Cam was my explosive ordinance specialist for six years. Best instincts with a bomb I've ever seen. Most snipers, though...they come back pretty wrecked." Too many of the guys I knew—not well, but enough to grab a beer off base once in a while—ended up committing suicide within a few years of retirement.

Her shoulders relax, and she sinks back in her chair. "I have a very good shrink. And a few coping mechanisms that...usually work." Inara's voice drops, and I have to strain to hear her. "The dead will haunt you if you let them. I can picture every one of my kills. Most of us can, I think. At least now, I get to choose when I pick up my gun and how I do my job. The ideal mission leaves the kidnappers unconscious or tied up, not dead. But it happens. West's first mission..."

"He told me you saved his life." She flinches. "I'm sorry. We don't have to talk about—"

Though her eyes have gone glassy, she waves her hand. "That mission was FUBAR from the time we touched down in Colombia. Bad intel. We're lucky we made it out of there at all. It was kill or be killed, and I have a very strong desire to stay alive."

She takes a long sip of her martini, the liquid in the glass shimmering as her hand trembles slightly. "Enough of that shit. We're supposed to be having fun. Ryker's a good guy. Smart, dedicated. With West running our ops, we're a solid team—even if the new guy does need some serious work on his rappelling skills. We train three nights a week. Work out together, run simulations. Keeps us on our toes. Once a month, I head out to Eastern Washington on the weekend for long-range target practice. My brother-in-law has fifty acres out near Wenatchee."

"Does that leave you any time for fun?"

Her laugh may be my new favorite sound—particularly when it clears the ghosts of the past from her eyes. "Not as much as I'd like, but I make time for what's important to me." With her fingers wrapped around the stem of her glass, she fixes me with an intense stare. "What about you?"

"I've got nothing but time right now." Flexing my left hand in my lap, I try to steel myself for my next words. Even though most people would never know it to look at me, the memories of being half-paralyzed haunt me every day. "I...uh...a few months ago—"

The petite server saves me, and we order enough food for at least four people before we're alone again and I struggle to figure out what to say.

"Royce," Inara says as she reaches across the table to touch my hand. "We don't need to talk about your...stroke...unless you want to."

I stare down at our hands as the warmth from her fingers seeps into my skin. If given the choice, I'd never mention it again. But that wouldn't be fair to me or to her. Inara needs to know what she's getting into before this goes any further than drinks and a few appetizers.

"I haven't really talked about it. With anyone. Except Cam. She and West...uh...basically moved in with me for two weeks after my surgery. Hell, he was still recovering from Columbia. But I was messed up enough that I couldn't be alone."

"Shit, Royce. I'm sorry."

For a split second, pity darkens her gaze, but she blinks, and it's gone, replaced by regret. She starts to pull her hand away, but I stop her, curling my fingers around hers. "I need to be blunt."

"Okay." She draws the word out, uncertain.

"When we exchanged numbers at West's the other night, I felt something. At the risk of sounding like a ss-stalker, I haven't been able to get you out of my head."

"You're not the only one who felt that way," she says quietly.

"Before this goes any further, you deserve to know what happened."

Twirling the olives around the mostly empty glass, I take a

deep breath. "Three years ago, I was diagnosed with a brain stem glioma. Basically, a benign tumor. At first, it wasn't too bad. Some nausea. Headaches. But then..." Can I really confess everything on our first date? The seizures? The personality changes? Mood swings? Anger? No. Not yet.

"Then?" Inara prompts, her brows arching subtly.

I take another sip of my martini. "Nine months ago, things got bad. I could barely get through the day. Trying to hold myself together at work, not let my family see how fucked up I was when I flew home for the fourth of July... My doctor gave me two options. Surgery, or let the damn thing kill me."

Inara

"For days after the surgery, I kept thinking it was all a dream. That I'd wake up and be able to talk. Or get out of bed." Memories haunt his eyes, and he fidgets with his napkin as our server slides a plate of roasted vegetables in between us. "Took me a week to manage more than the easiessst sounds. More than a month to walk."

"Royce—" I don't know what to say. I'm shit at offering comfort, and I don't think he wants it. Or needs it. But staying silent doesn't feel right either. "I couldn't tell. At West's the other night."

He forces a smile and runs a hand through his hair. "Cam ordered me around a lot the first month. They didn't expect her to walk again after the bombs. Hell, they almossst took her leg. I...wasn't there, but the other guys in the unit kept me updated. She fought for every step. Then she had to do it all over again —with me."

His control slips, just for a moment, and raw anguish tightens lines around his eyes and lips. But just as quickly, he slides the mask back into place and puts it away.

"Even when she was at Emerald City for fifteen hours a day, she'd send me emails. Demanding I get up, take a loop around my condo. Or she'd call and make me recite one of the tongue twiss-twisters my therapist gave me. And...it worked."

He smiles, and I melt a little. I can hear the stutters now. The long "s" sound as he tries to form certain words. And when I took his arm, needing someone to hold onto after my little flashback in my car, I thought his gait was a little uneven.

Worry tingles along my spine. "I always thought strokes happened to...older people."

Royce drops his gaze to the plate of vegetables between us. "Me too. Turns out, one of the meds I was on before surgery can sometimes cause blood clots. I had a brain scan last week. No tumor, no clots."

He says it almost like he's trying to prove something to me, and shame heats the back of my neck. I'm about to apologize when his voice takes on a rough edge.

"I guess you could call me lucky. There's no proof, but a couple guys in my unit had similar growths. Lungs, liver. My doc is pretty sure we were all exposed to something during our last tour that caused this."

"Cam too?" I don't know her well, but with how West talked about her when he drove me home the other night, something like this could kill him.

Royce drains his water glass. "Different tour." With an uncomfortable pinch to his features, he clears his throat. "After Cam was injured, I joined another unit. Chemical weapons disposal."

"Shit. We always used to think those guys were insane," I say. "And *my* unit broke into Hell."

Glancing at his empty martini glass, Royce sighs. "You aren't wrong. But that's...a story for another time. With a lot more alcohol."

"I don't have anywhere to be." I smile and finish off my drink. With a quick glance at my watch, I add, "And I still have three hours until pumpkin time."

Royce laughs, and the demons that haunted his eyes as he recounted his diagnosis, the surgery, and waking up unable to speak or move shift into something darker. He signals the server, and we order another round, but when she rushes off to the bar, he settles back in his chair.

"I was pretty messed up after Cam was hurt. The bombs didn't touch me beyond a single piece of shrapnel." He gestures to a long scar on his forearm. "But this was my team. I didn't know how to go back. So I went to my CO and requested the most dangerous, fucked-up assignment he could give me. Said it was either that or I was out."

I clench my fists under the table. Even now, years later, I can see the pain in Royce's eyes. "And your CO listened to you?"

He shrugs. "I didn't give him much of a choice. Command needed a team leader for a chemical weapons disposal unit, and I jumped at it. Got the hell out of Bagram and threw myself into the work."

The last of our appetizers sits forgotten between us, and I worry I've lost him to his memories. But then the next round of drinks arrives, and he forces a smile. "Enough of my shit for a while. Why did you decide to become a sniper?"

Turnabout's fair play, I suppose, and watching Royce battle some of his demons—and win—gives me hope I can do the same. I tuck a curl behind my ear. "My mother was born in Iran. She legally immigrated to the United States a couple of years before the Shah went into exile. Her brothers, though, stayed. We heard stories of the protests, and once the Ayatollah Khomeini took power, communication...was difficult. She worried so much for them. Still does. Uncle Ebrahem got out ten years ago and the stories he told... He lives in London now."

"How old was your mother?" We order dessert, and I twirl the olives around in my martini glass.

"Nineteen. She worked as a flight attendant, and met my father, a British diplomat, not long after the hostages were released. Both of them agreed that the world was not the place they'd thought it to be."

My mother's scream echoes in my memories, and I shake my head to banish the sight of her blood pooling on the sidewalk. Digging my short nails into my palms, I fight for control. "They taught me languages, and by the time I was fifteen, I spoke English, German, Persian, and French fluently."

Royce's mouth forms an *o,* and he sits back in his chair. "All I could ever manage was a little broken Pashto." He offers me the last slice of prosciutto, and the time allows me to reflect on just how few people I've told my story to. My platoon knew most of it. But...when your heritage includes one of the nations your army is fighting *against*, you keep a lot of that shit to yourself.

"I took two years of college classes, but then my father had a heart attack." I clear my throat, refusing to let my control slip. "Between the medical bills and his...death, money was tight. So, I took a leave of absence and joined the army. I thought...I could make a difference."

Royce nods, and I wonder where our similarities end. "I had to prove myself. Both as a woman and as an Iranian. Even though I was born here, my name, my skin color, the shape of my eyes... they brand me. The hazing never let up."

My voice cracks, though I won't go back there. Some of the worst days of my life. Even worse than the past few months. Royce reaches across the table, and his warm fingers caress my wrist. Forcing myself to meet his gaze, I take a deep breath. "In the third phase of basic, I left everyone in the dust on the qualifications course. Forty targets. I hit thirty-nine of them. Next best guy on the course took out thirty."

"Shit. I only managed twenty-seven. Barely passed." Respect tinges his voice, and I let myself smile.

"After that, the abuse died down. Hell, most of the guys were afraid of me. My CO put me in for sniper training the next day."

Something in his touch soothes me, and I turn my hand to link our fingers. "Now that we've both shared some of the messy stuff...what do you like to do for fun?"

Two hours later, Royce and I huddle under the overhang outside the bar. A light rain slicks the city streets, and the scent of the sea hangs in the air. "I don't want to let you go," he says as he pulls me close. "When can I see you again?"

I run my hands down his strong chest. "I have training tomorrow, but Friday? Dinner? And...maybe..."

"Breakfast on Saturday?" His voice is suddenly rough, and as I mold myself to his lean frame, something inside me warms. When he cups my ass, my core clenches, need driving me up to my toes so I can press my lips to his.

He tastes of the chocolate cake and espresso we shared, and when he deepens the kiss, his tongue seeking mine, I let him take. Royce tangles his fingers in my hair, pulling hard enough to send tiny pinpricks of pain along my scalp.

I push him back against the wall, and he angles my head, his lips traveling along my jaw, back to my ear, and down to the curve of my neck. "Oh God," I whisper as my knees weaken. "Yes. Breakfast."

If we weren't in public, I'd cup his rather obvious erection through his black jeans and grind myself against him. But modesty prevails as the Lyft driver pulls up to the curb and gives the horn a quick tap.

Royce pulls away, silver flecks sparkling in his blue eyes. "Text me when you get home?"

"I will."

He waits until I get my bearings before he lets me go, and the absence of his warmth leaves me wanting as he walks slowly backward towards the car. "Rest up, pumpkin," he says with a wink. "Friday night, you're mine."

I wait until he shuts the car door before I whisper, "All yours."

6

Inara

MY SHOES KICK up splatters of water as I push myself through a grueling five-mile run—complete with a monster hill on Phinney Ridge—and when I reach the top, I rest my hands on my thighs and try not to wheeze. Something shifted in the air last night, and I'll be surprised if it doesn't snow before the end of the day. My lungs burn, and there's a harsh edge to the air. Not yet 5:00 a.m. and the sun hasn't peeked over the Cascades. The streetlights cast shimmering shadows on the rain-slicked pavement.

Once I can breathe again, I start jogging the last few blocks to my neighborhood coffee shop. The Daily Bean doesn't brew the best coffee in Seattle—hell, West probably wouldn't be caught dead here—but they know my name and my preference for a quad-shot Americano after my morning runs. Plus, they donate a portion of their proceeds every Saturday to the local battered women's shelter.

I roll my head around and crack my neck as I wait for the light to change so I can cross the street. Thoughts of Royce—and the final kiss we shared—woke me more than once, and now I wonder just how I'm going to make it until tomorrow feeling this…needy. I haven't dated anyone in more than five years. I didn't know how much you could miss human touch. I want him. But at the same time, I hate this feeling. This ache inside me for a man who seems to get me—and who might understand why I feel so out of my element.

Tires squeal, an engine revs, and I spin around just in time to see a black SUV barreling towards me, fishtailing on the slick roads.

I react—training taking over—and jump back, but the large electrical box behind me stops my momentum with a bone-jarring crack of my hip against metal. The SUV's almost on top of me, and I scream, "Stop!" as I try to make my throbbing right leg work. The electrical box saves me once I grab the top of it and haul myself up. The SUV jumps the curb and passes me with only inches to spare.

"You fucking asshole!" I scream. I'm too slow pulling my phone from my pocket—plus my hands are shaking too much to take a photo—and I only saw two digits of the license number.

Corrine, the morning barista, races across the street. "Oh my God. Are you okay?"

I'm still crouched on top of the electrical box, shaking, and when she repeats her question, and I can't form words to answer her, I realize I might not be.

Corrine slides her arm around my waist and lets me use her shoulders for leverage as I half-climb, half-fall to the ground. My legs won't quite support me.

"N-not hurt," I manage. "Just…shaken up. Give me…a minute."

"That asshole could have killed you." She shakes her head, and messy curls tumble around her heart-shaped face. "The drunk drivers on this street have been getting worse and worse the past few months. There's an illegal bar that moves around the ridge—mostly out of people's garages—and they keep serving until 6:00 a.m."

"Fuckers." I can't manage anything more complex yet, but I let Corrine help me to my feet and walk me over to the coffee shop. She sits me down, gets her coat from the back, and wraps the fleece around my shoulders.

"I'll call the police and then get you a coffee, okay?"

I nod, my heart still racing. Closing my eyes, I let Corrine's murmur lull me into a semi-trance as I pull my mantra from the depths of my mind. *Breathe, believe, act. Breathe, believe, act. Breathe, believe act.* By the time the coffee grinder starts, I can no longer hear my heartbeat thundering in my ears, but that might be worse. Now, I'm wondering why it took me so long to move, why I spent so long just *staring* at the vehicle speeding towards me.

The scent of my usual drink calms me, and I force my eyes open to meet Corrine's concerned gaze. "How're you doing, hon?"

She slides an orange cranberry scone in front of me, and I try to force a smile in thanks.

"Been better. I was in the army for ten years. You'd think I could handle a crisis a little better." I take a sip of the dark brew and shudder as I try to stop my tears from spilling over.

"You can't prepare for something like that. It's just so random."

Another customer pushes through the door, and I nod towards the coffee bar. "I'm okay. How long 'til the cops show up?"

"Ten minutes or so. You just relax."

With my coffee and comforting carbs within reach, I let my head rest against the wall behind me. Relax. Sure. Because I've always been so good at that.

By the time I deal with the police, my hip goes from numb to screaming pain. Thank God for car-sharing. The four-block walk to my tiny rental house would have taken me all fucking day. A handful of ibuprofen should get me through work—after all, I don't have to do much more than sit at my desk, but the thought of one of Ryker's grueling workout sessions makes me shudder.

A hot shower helps, though catching sight of the blooming purple bruise covering my left hip makes me cringe, and I start to tremble again. I've had bombs dropped so close to my location I had to open my mouth before impact or my lungs would have burst from the percussive force, and one drunk driver is reducing me to a quivering mess. I sink down to the floor and let the hot water rush over me as I drop my head into my hands.

In war, there's an element of control. Or...at least convention. No, the enemy doesn't always play fair. But armies have habits and routines you can anticipate. This? One step in the wrong direction, one extra second of delay, and I would have died. Or ended up in the hospital with serious injuries. I was lucky. Someone without my training wouldn't have been.

On my way to work, I engage the hands-free and call Royce. I wish I could see him, feel his arms around me. We ended last night in bed—on the phone of course—trading suggestions of what we wanted to do to one another. A little of that might take the edge off my raw mood.

"'Morning," he says with just a hint of a Texas drawl. Sleep still lingers in his voice, and I kick myself as I realize it's not even eight yet.

"Oh shit. I woke you up, didn't I?" A city bus cuts me off, and I swear and lay on the horn.

A yawn stretches over the line. "Maybe. But I can only think of one better way to wake up, and you're not here, so..."

"Pretend I am."

"I'd open my eyes to see you straddling me. Your hands

sliding down my chest. Oh, and you're naked. I wrap my hands around your hips, and your scent..."

My eyelids flutter, and as the stoplight turns green, I clear my throat. "Maybe this was a bad idea. I'm going to run off the road."

"There are some advantages to taking a car service everywhere." His throaty laugh is infectious, and as I try to maneuver the rental car down one of Seattle's narrower side streets, I think maybe he's right. I miss my coupe.

"Doing anything fun today?" We're still in the early stages of this "thing" between us, and while I could listen to his voice all day, I've never been very good at small talk.

"Working on my app. I have a meeting with Cam on Monday, and I want everything polished so she can decide if it's something she wants to integrate into Oversight."

"Isn't that your decision? You still own Emerald City, don't you?"

"For now." A hint of strain darkens his voice. "I'm seeing my lawyer next week. He'll draw up the sale paperwork. Cam's done a kick-ass job, and she deserves to run the place. Permanently. If she wants, I'll take an advisory position, draw a small salary. But almost dying helps you see what's important. I ran a good business. Hired great people. Even worked some killer deals. But Cam...she's a natural. And this app...it has real potential to help people."

Turning down Seneca, I sigh as the sparkling waters of Puget Sound stretch out before me. Sometimes I forget how beautiful this city is.

"You okay?" Movement carries over the line, and I think I hear a coffee grinder in the background.

"Almost at work. Parking sucks down by the water, but at least I get to see Puget Sound every morning. Kind of wish you were here with me."

"Are you okay, baby?"

My breath hitches at the term of endearment and the care I

hear in his voice. Am I? Probably not, but he's there, and I'm here, and what's wrong with me he can't fix.

"Fine. I…just didn't sleep well. I swear, I'm not usually this…needy."

"Tomorrow night, I plan on needing you multiple times." His husky tone sends my heart racing and almost makes me forget about the drunk driver and Coop's death.

We chat about the weather, about how awesome my mechanic is to have my car ready for me this afternoon, and where we want to eat tomorrow night. "I should go," I say as I park and throw my door open. Standing, though, proves more difficult than I'd anticipated, and I hiss out a breath when my hip protests the movement. Damn. Sitting for half an hour didn't do me any favors.

"Inara? What's wrong?"

I should tell him, but he'll worry, and there's nothing he can do. So I hedge.

"I fell on my run this morning. I'm fine. Just a little banged up. Getting out of the car hurt more than I expected."

"Why don't we stay in tomorrow? I'll cook. Come over at seven."

A single bruise won't keep me down, but I'm still jetlagged, and a quiet dinner with Royce—followed by some not-so-quiet sex is what the doctor would order. "Deal. I'll bring the wine. Red or white?"

"Red." After a pause, he clears his throat. "I hope you like spicy."

The rough edge to his tone hints at more than food, and I chuckle. "Bring it on, soldier. I can handle spicy."

Royce

*Waves of heat shimmer above the sand, and I rub the back of my neck
with my gloved hand. My back aches, and my stomach roils. I should
have put an end to the drinking before 2:00 a.m., but no one's had a
break in weeks.*

*A thousand yards away, Cam crouches in front of a bomb strapped
to a piece of playground equipment. "Come on, baby," she says quietly
over comms. "Tell me all your secrets."*

*"Rolls." Yanko kneels next to me. We're crouched behind a concrete
wall, our six-man team—well, five men and Cam—all exhausted. We
weren't even supposed to be on duty today, but the other ordinance unit
has food poisoning. All of them. Fucking luck of the draw.*

"What?" I hiss. "She's almost done. Don't distract her."

*"Something's wrong. That burned out car next to her? It wasn't
there yesterday. SAT scans—"*

"Almost got her," Cam says.

*"Sergeant, listen. Special Forces lost a three-man team last week.
Same sort of deal. A pile of debris that wasn't there the day before...
bombs hidden under pressure plates and too much sand and metal to be
detected by our equipment."*

*Yanko's a worrier, and Cam's about done, so I hold up my hand in
dismissal.*

*Cam brushes her hands on her suit. "I have the detonator; headed
for you."*

*"You're clear," I say even as Yanko grabs my arm. I'm ready to tear
him a new one until I see his face. That's not worry. That's pure terror.
"Pint, stop!"*

*The first explosion sends my heart into my throat. The second tears
a scream free, and the third sends Cam's slight frame flying. The rest of
the bombs detonate in slow motion, but I don't see or hear them. I'm
focused on her. She isn't moving.*

Ignoring Yanko trying to hold me back, I vault over the wall and race for her. I don't care if there are more bombs. Once I hear her choked cry, I'm unstoppable.

"Call for evac!" I scream as I climb over the mangled playground equipment to reach her. "Cam, don't move!"

Her suit's burned, the thick material melting into her skin. Shrapnel's shredded her arm, and her left leg is broken in at least two places. Blood gushes from her side, and I press my hands to the wound. I can't see her face. Her helmet still covers her face, though there's a massive dent in one side. Yanko reaches us and tears the helmet off before I can stop him.

"What the fuck? She could have a spinal cord injury!" One look at her face, though, and I know she can feel every burn, break, and gash. "Pint, hold on. MEDEVAC is on their way." With a quick glance up at Yanko, I confirm he's called them, and the rest of the team gathers around us.

"Rolls," she whispers as her eyelids flutter. "Don't leave me."

"I've got you. But you have to hold on, Cam. It's not that bad. Once they patch up your side and your leg, you'll be fine."

"Don't...lie." A drop of blood escapes her lips. When she coughs, her entire body spasms. "Tell...my family...find...them...so sorry...love..."

"Shut up, soldier. That's an order. You are not going to die. Do you hear me? Keep those eyes open and focus on me."

The whoop, whoop, whoop of the MEDEVAC sounds like it's miles away, and I press my hands harder against Cam's stomach. "Fight. Please, fight."

I land on the floor with a bone-jarring thud, and when I open my eyes, I'm in my living room staring up at my couch.

After yoga, I wanted to dive right into my app, but then the Alzheimer's Association of Seattle called. I have to be at my best to meet with them this afternoon, so I'd stretched out on the sofa with some meditative music streaming from my phone.

I'm luckier than most. My nightmares and PTSD aren't that bad. But whenever I dream—and remember—it's always that terrible day when Cam almost died because I hesitated.

I drive the heels of my hands into my eyes, trying to force away the sight of all the blood, her suit melting into her arm, and her mangled leg. I tried to stop the bleeding, kept her alive her until the MEDEVAC touched down, then held her hand the whole flight to the military hospital. Talked to her. Made her answer me.

And then…I left her. Sure, I waited around long enough for the doctors to tell me that she'd live, but after that, I left Yanko in charge, got piss drunk, and didn't leave the barracks for three days.

My team took shifts at her bedside. I didn't even ask about her. I couldn't. Between finding more bourbon—not the good stuff—and wondering how the hell I could live with myself after that mistake, let alone face her again, I retreated into a shell, ignored everyone who came to check on me, and didn't emerge until I went to my CO a week later to beg for reassignment.

I stumble into the shower, my head pounding. I thought I'd moved past the worst of the guilt. Or…at least shoved it so deep down inside me that it couldn't affect me. After all, Cam and I are talking again. Though since I only opened up to her a few weeks before my surgery, the conversation was largely one-sided for a while. Hard to explain yourself when you can't talk.

She forgave me—though I still don't know why. But seeing her the other day when West was gone…it was clear the damage I caused with my cowardice hasn't healed. In fact, if West *is* getting ready to propose or ask her to move in with him again, it's going to hit her all over again.

Dammit. We have to have a serious talk. Soon.

My tie itches. This is Seattle, for fuck's sake. The only people wearing ties in this city are bankers and hotel desk clerks. But I need this meeting to go well, so I dug out the power-blue noose and fumbled through tying it for half an hour. Post-stroke Royce might need to invest in clip-ons.

"Mr. Nadiri?" The woman standing in front of me looks like a cross between my grandmother and Maggie Smith in the *Harry Potter* movies. Dressed to the nines, a high-necked blouse buttoned all the way up, with her gray hair pulled back in a severe bun. But her smile welcomes me, and her eyes crinkle with warmth as she shakes my hand. "I'm Minerva."

Of course.

"A pleasure, Minerva. Thanks for seeing me this afternoon."

She gestures to a small conference room off the lobby of the Alzheimer's Association's Seattle headquarters. "We're in here. I'm very excited to see how Loc8tion works and hear about your plans for the future. Can I get you some coffee while you set up?"

"That would be great. Thank you." I pull out my laptop as Minerva clips out of the room on high-heeled lace-up boots.

By the time she returns with two steaming cups of coffee, I have my presentation ready to go.

"I hope you don't mind. I invited my CIO to join us," she says as a tall, severe man in a crisp black suit joins us.

"Leo Haight," he says as we shake hands. "Let's see what you've got."

"Loc8tion is a GPS-enabled app designed to help those who struggle with directions, memory, or distances. In its current version, it allows the administrative user to track any other users on the system with a few keystrokes. If a user gets lost, the admin can scroll through their last eight stops and Loc8tion will give them directions."

As I run through the demo, Leo and Minerva nod at all of the appropriate places, asking intelligent questions about the app's functionality, and exchanging what I think are impressed glances.

"Currently, the app requires an iPhone or Android device and a smartwatch, but I'm working with hardware manufacturers to see if the tracker can be embedded in a pendant, belt buckle, or bracelet. I hope in the future, I can work with the Medic-Alert company to create a bracelet or pendant or medallion that would combine a user's Medic-Alert status and my transmitter."

"That's wonderful," Minerva says. "And the cost per user?"

"Retail, the software alone will go for $3.99. But that's just for the standalone version. Administrative capabilities are $49.99 for up to ten users. Additional users can be added in packages of ten for $9.99."

"And the devices?"

"I'm afraid I don't have a cost for those yet. But the initial estimates are coming in at around fifty dollars if I order under a thousand, twenty-five dollars if I order more than five thousand."

Minerva nods, her enthusiasm growing. "So for approximately one hundred dollars, a family could have peace of mind that their loved one could always be found."

"Well, as long as the loved one was somewhere with a GPS signal. But even if they wandered into the bus tunnel, the system would record the last known GPS tower ping, so they'd have a reasonable idea."

"What do you need from us?" She folds her hands on the table, leaning forward.

"Honestly, at the moment, I'd love to have you test the system and potentially give Loc8tion an endorsement when we launch. I'm not asking for money—not that I'd turn it down."

We all chuckle, and Minerva nods. "I'd be happy to give it a trial run. Do you know when you'll have a non-watch receiver ready for testing?"

"Potentially within the next month. My first test units came last week, and I have several others from different companies arriving tomorrow."

"Excellent. I'd like to try both the watch version and the receiver version before we commit to endorsing, but I'm very impressed with the possibilities and peace of mind this could give our families."

"If you wouldn't mind signing this non-disclosure agreement," I say as I withdraw a folder from my briefcase, "I can walk you through the installation and configuration of the basic app right now."

"I'll take those," Leo says. "Just want to give them a quick once-over. I'm sure you understand."

I nod. "Wouldn't have it any other way."

While he reads, Minerva takes me on a tour of their offices. "Most of the people who work here have had Alzheimer's touch their lives in some way. My husband was diagnosed four years ago. He's done well. I have a caregiver, but he's still at home, and we have nights where it doesn't seem like he's sick at all. Others... I live with a stranger."

"I'm sorry." I shove my hands into my pockets as she shows me the course for their next charity 5k race.

"Why did you develop this app, Mr. Nadiri?"

"Royce, please." *Shit. She had to ask.* After a deep breath, I force myself to meet her gaze. "I had a stroke three months ago. I was lucky. It didn't affect my memory. But during rehab, I met several other men and women who were fighting their way back. One in particular, an older guy, avid runner, lost his short-term memory completely. Probably for good. He'd had to stop running outside because he kept getting lost.

"When I served in the army, I knew too many guys with traumatic brain injuries who had the same sort of issues. They'd get confused. Leave their homes, head to the grocery store, then forget how to get back again. I spent a solid month barely able to walk. But, I could use the computer. Decided to do something more productive than just binge on Netflix. Once I started coding, I couldn't stop."

Minerva looks me up and down. "You seem to have made a full recovery."

"'Bout ninety percent. Loc8tion gave me a purpose. That, along with a couple of good friends and some kick-ass...err, highly talented therapists got me where I am today."

By now, we've reached the conference room once more, and Leo waves us back inside. "Nothing out of the ordinary. Go ahead and sign, Minerva. Mr. Nadiri, it was a pleasure to meet you. I look forward to hearing Minerva's impressions of Loc8tion." With a quick, but firm handshake, Leo strides from the room.

Once Minerva pens her flowing signature, I gesture to the chair across from me. "Okay. First thing I need is your phone."

7

Inara

AT PRECISELY SEVEN, I pull my coupe into a parking space outside
Hidden Agenda. "I missed you, baby," I say as I pat her dash-
board. "I'll never cheat on you again."

Before I head inside, I grab a couple ibuprofen from the
glovebox and wash them down with a swig from my water bottle.
I really don't want to go into the whole "almost hit by a car" thing
before our training session tonight. Not that Ryker would go easy
on me or anything. Dude's a great leader. But he can be a real
dick when he's in a mood.

As I slip through the door, I give West a mock-salute. He's
stretching next to the boxing ring with Graham hanging from the
pull-up bar by his legs, powering through crunches. Both men
are shirtless, and though I have nothing but platonic feelings for
both of them, I stare for a brief second—I'm not dead after all,
and they're both cut like you wouldn't believe.

And then my mind wanders to what I think Royce might look
like without a shirt, and something in my core flutters. Sure, the

men I work with could be *Men's Health* models, but they don't do much of anything for me. Royce does.

If Ryker allowed phones inside, I'd probably text Royce a shot of me in my sports bra right now. Maybe with my hand halfway down my tight running shorts.

"Best of three in the ring?" West calls as he snags a bottle of water from the mini-fridge in the corner.

"Need to loosen up first," I say, gesturing to the climbing wall. "Race you to the top?" I toss a glance to Graham. "New guy. Let's see those climbing skills!"

West wins—of course—but I beat Graham, who loses his grip halfway up and lets the harness catch him.

"How the hell do you guys manage to never miss a hold?" He's panting when West and I drop to the ground, and I gesture to the wall.

"Again. Follow my lead."

Ryker, who watched our race with a gleam of respect in his eyes, heads for the boxing ring with West while I take Graham through a difficult path up the wall. He follows, and once we've descended, I make him lead for round three. After ten feet, he stops. Glancing around wildly, he starts to panic.

"Deep breaths. Focus, Peck. You're better than this. Remember. The best path isn't always up." I hang five feet off the ground by one handhold and one foothold. My hip aches, but I'm powering through the pain.

Graham scans the wall from side to side. I'm about to tell him to look down when he spies the outcropping he needs. Dropping his right hand ten inches, he scouts for a lower foothold. Soon, he's moved three feet to the right and is steadily rising once more.

At the top, I pause to give him a high-five before pushing off the wall and letting the belay line catch me. "Take ten—no peeking over here. I'm going to rearrange some of the holds, and you can try again."

Graham salutes before he runs over to the kitchen for an

energy drink. Swinging over empty air, I blow out a deep breath. All night, my nerves have been on overdrive. I'm half-tempted to ping Royce when I'm done and see if he can help me spend this frenetic energy, but the last text I received said he was going to bed early after some big meeting he had downtown.

Ryker climbs two feet up the wall and starts unlocking various hand and footholds, swapping them out with lightning speed. I mirror his movements from the top, and we meet a little over halfway up.

"One to ten?" he asks.

"Eight." I'm sore, and I can't shake the slight tremors in my fingers. But my hip isn't giving me much trouble and being here helps center me.

"I'm taking West on an in-and-out tomorrow. Intel retrieval. No live targets. Infiltration only." Ryker glances over at me as I tighten the last handhold. "You want to hang here with 'new guy'? He's going to monitor our comms."

"Nope. I'm booked tomorrow night." I try to hide my smile, but Ryker didn't stay alive for close to two years in Hell without being one of the most observant men on the planet.

He raises a brow. "So, you're getting serious with the geek."

"Hey. He's not..." The absurdity of my protest hits me, and I start to laugh. "Okay, fine. He's a geek. But he 'gets' me."

Letting the belay line out slowly, I float to the ground. Ryker lands with a grunt next to me. "You and West both." He shakes his head. "What we do... I'll never count on growing old with someone."

"Ry—" I let my hand drop as he shoots me a look exposing the darkness that lives inside him. "We're not that serious. Just having fun." My verbal one-eighty feels all wrong, but Ryker nods, then turns on his heel and walks away. Fuck. Right about now, the no cell phone rule really chafes. Because all I want to do is call Royce.

Not that serious? Who am I kidding? I'm falling for the guy.

Right about now, my little coupe isn't doing me any favors. After training last night, I collapsed onto my bed at 10:00 p.m. without the ice pack I knew I needed. Today, I'm hurting. Sitting at my desk was pure torture. Now, as I pull my sleek, little white convertible into a parking spot a block from Royce's condo, I'm dreading getting out of the car.

But the idea of dinner—and more—with Royce fortifies me against the momentary agony. Stupid, really. Had I taken the previous night off—actually *told* Ryker that I'd hurt myself—I'd probably feel a lot better today.

My heartbeat quickens as I knock on Royce's door. A date shouldn't affect me like this, but it's been so long since I spent the night with anyone other than my teammates, and all of *those* nights involved bugs, bullets, and blood.

Oh God.

Royce smiles as he stands in the open door, and something inside me melts a little. Or a lot. Dark denim hugs his hips. A blue Henley sets off his eyes, and though he's not as bulky as West or Ryker, the shirt highlights his chest and his biceps nicely. The scents of rich tobacco, cloves, and cedar surround me as he pulls me in for a hug.

When he reaches down to cup my ass, though, his fingers dig into the bruise on my hip, and I can't stifle my whimper.

"What's wrong?" He doesn't let me go but holds me at arm's length, his gaze traveling up and down my body. "Are you in pain? Oh shit. When you fell yesterday? That's still hurting you?"

I try to slip by him, put a little distance between the two of us before I answer, and he lets me, but once he's closed the door, he pins me against the wall. "You're avoiding the question."

"No. Just trying to forget the answer. Wine?" I hold up the

bottle, but he slides the Merlot from my hand and deposits it on a table next to the door.

"Inara."

I splay my hands against his chest, relishing his warmth. "I didn't exactly fall. More like slammed my whole body into an electrical box."

"Why?"

"Trying to avoid a stupid drunk who didn't care about sidewalks. Nothing's broken."

Royce wraps his arm around my waist as he leads me into his living room and I swear he supports my weight as we sink down onto his black leather couch. He doesn't let go as I tell him about the SUV, then pull down the waistband of my pants to show him the top of the bruise that covers my hip. "The cops can't do anything. With only two digits of the license number, they'll probably never find the guy."

"You were damn lucky." He nudges my chin up, and his touch brands my skin. I can't help but lean closer, and when our lips meet, I don't care how much it hurts. I want him. His breath whispers across my cheek. When he nibbles my lower lip, I shudder.

Coming up for air, I whisper, "You're the best pain reliever ever." Already slick with need, I try to lift the Henley. "Fuck me, Royce."

"I could hurt you. And there's dinner...soon." He tries to pull away, but I'm relentless, and the shirt lands on the back of the couch.

"You won't. And unless you're making a soufflé..."

He stills my hands. "Inara..." A sigh almost deflates him. "I haven't been with anyone in a long time." Uncertainty laces his tone, and when I meet his gaze, fear churns in the depths of his eyes.

"Pretty sure the basics haven't changed."

He doesn't respond to my joke, and I dip my head to press a kiss to the hollow of his throat. I trail my lips lower, across his collarbone. "I don't know," I say as I run my hands over his chest, the light sprinkling of dark hair tickling my fingers, "why anyone with a body like yours would be nervous." Though he's thin, he's toned, wiry and cut, with a definite six pack I suspect will turn into eight once I get his pants off. And I *will* get his pants off.

"Inara," he groans as I palm his erection through his jeans. "Fuck."

"That's the idea." I tease his nipple with my teeth, and he pushes me back against the cushions, pinning my wrists over my head.

"Are you sure?" His eyes flash dangerously now, his voice gritty and hoarse. "I...don't do gentle."

"Neither do I." Testing his grip, I find I can't escape, and I grin as I wriggle my hips against his. There's only a little pain now, endorphins taking over, and I part my legs, one of his firm thighs pressing against my mound. "There's...a condom in my purse."

His eyebrows arch, and with his free hand, he extracts not one, but three foil packets from his back pocket. "I might be nervous, but I wasn't going to be unprepared."

"My kind of man."

With a low rumble in his throat, he drops the packets on the floor, then palms my breast. My nipple rises under his touch, and I arch my back. The silk tank lets his thumb slide easily, and when he pinches—first a light tease, then with enough force to make me gasp—the pleasure zings directly to my clit.

"Off with this," he orders and pulls me up. The tank sails to the floor. "You didn't strike me as a lace fan." He fondles my nipple through my bra. "But I like it." As he sucks and bites, words fail me. Pinning my hands on either side of my head, he covers me with his long, lean body. I didn't even realize he'd unbuttoned my pants, but my wriggling has exposed my utterly soaked lace thong, and I don't know how much longer I can hold on.

"Harder," I gasp and try to get just a little more friction

between us. Royce obliges, and when he grinds his hips into me and then switches his focus to my other breast, I implode, his name on my lips as waves of pleasure overtake me.

When I can breathe again, he's staring down at me with a slightly dazed look on his face. I probably should have warned the poor man how easily I get off. But my release only stoked my desire further, and I pull a hand free to pop open the top button of his jeans. "Don't worry; I'm nowhere near done."

The challenge in my tone lights a fire in his gaze, and sparks of silver deepen in his blue eyes. I loosen another button. Royce captures my hand and brings my palm to his lips. "How good are you at following orders?"

I shiver. "As long as I get what I want, pretty good, soldier. Which right now, is you. Naked."

He pushes to his feet, and the loss of his body heat raises gooseflesh on my bare skin. But when Royce toes off his shoes, then shoves his jeans down his hips to reveal a pair of black briefs, my desire burns so hot, I think I might catch fire.

"Turn so you're sitting with your feet on the floor, spread your legs, and hold on to the back of the couch, arms over your head. Then don't move." Royce towers over me, all six-foot-four inches of him coiled and ready to spring, hands on his hips as he ensures I follow his commands.

The thrill of a man who understands my needs has me half-panting, and when he gently pulls my pants down my hips, the tenderness of his touch makes it hard to swallow over the lump in my throat.

"Fuck, baby. I don't want to hurt you."

His gaze burns into my hip, and I only spare a single glance at the dark purple, black, and green bruise. "I can take a little pain."

As my dual meaning sinks in, he drops to his knees, his cock already standing at attention. My thong slides away next, and then—oh fuck. His tongue flicks my sensitive nub, and I dig my nails into the couch cushion, the leather smooth against my fingers.

"God, Inara...you..." He dives in again, this time using his teeth, and pain and pleasure war with one another for dominance. "You're so," he thrusts two fingers inside of me, "fucking wet."

"More," I manage, and try to push my hips closer. Royce slaps the inside of my thigh, the slight sting the only warning I need not to move again. "Please."

"Oh, you'll get more." He grabs my legs behind my knees, pulls until my ass is almost hanging off the couch. My arms stretch to their limit, and I try not to wriggle when he seals his lips over my clit. With a growl, he sucks, hard, and I can't hold back.

My second climax carries me higher than the first, and I buck against him, biting my lip hard enough to draw blood so I don't end up screaming. He laps at my folds, drinking me in, and all I can think of is his cock inside me, his hands in my hair, and his lips on mine.

The crinkle of foil barely registers as I try to ride the seemingly endless waves of my release. But then he nudges my entrance, and I force my eyes open. "Royce."

With a single move, he plunges deep, and unused to his girth, I cry out. He stills, watching my face for signs he's hurt me, but I manage a single word. "Harder."

The couch starts to rock as he slams into me over and over, and when we've found our rhythm, his lips curve. "Grab my ass, baby."

I want to touch him, to run my hands along his corded arms, to feel his lips on mine. I start with his shoulders, scraping my short nails along his smooth skin, leaving faint red traces along his biceps, across his back, and finally, I squeeze his ass with everything I've got left. He claims my mouth, my release still on his lips and tongue. Our bodies in tune, another wave of pleasure swamps me just as his cock swells even more, and his abs start to quiver.

"Oh God," Royce groans, and I hold on for dear life as we fly over the edge together.

Royce

All day, I tried to talk myself out of this date. *You're too damaged. Too fucking thin. You're shit at being gentle. This is a bad idea. You're going to scare her.*

But now… Inara might be the perfect woman. Under me, she tries to catch her breath, and I come back to my senses.

Get off her, you ass.

"Sorry," I murmur as I withdraw and pinch off the condom. "I'll be right back."

Heading for my bathroom, the pins and needles in my left leg —the ones I live with every day, surge, but I manage to keep my gait steady. My knees burn; the rug probably took off at least two layers of skin, but I don't care. Once I toss the condom, I run a cloth under hot water and then return to Inara. Lowering myself down next to her, I try for tender as I gently swipe the cloth over her thighs, wincing at the reddish finger marks I left.

"Did I hurt you?" My hand hovers over her bruised hip, and she meets my gaze, an exhausted smile curving her lips.

"I feel better than I have all day." She slides her arm around my waist and pulls me down next to her. "Except, you were right. We should have eaten first."

She's as sex-drunk as I am, and I chuckle. "The night's still young."

"And I want to see your software and hear about the meeting

89

you had yesterday." With her head nestled on my shoulder, she swings her legs up over mine and quirks her brows. "Then, maybe later, we can have a hardware demonstration again."

"Where did you come from?" I rub her back, finding chilled skin, then shift to snag my shirt from the floor. "Put this on."

"Washington, D.C.," she says as she tugs the shirt over her head. "Also, what were you worried about? That was...wow."

My cheeks flame, but my chest swells with pride. "I haven't been with anyone in...three years. After a while, you start to worry you've lost your touch. And my preferences lie a little outside the vanilla realm."

"Women should be throwing themselves at you. Of course, now, I'd have to kick their asses if they tried." Inara brushes a kiss to my jaw. "Why didn't you date after your diagnosis?"

"You remember those pills I dropped at Cam's last week?"

"Yes." A wary edge creeps into her voice.

I tip her chin up so I can hold her gaze. "I didn't tell you everything the other night. I had my first seizure three years ago. Passed out, and when I came to, I couldn't talk for twenty minutes. Scared the fuck out of me. I was alone. In the kitchen. Making dinner. I don't know how I managed to set the knife down before I fell. Or how I missed cracking my head open on the cabinet."

Sympathy softens her features, and I rush to continue, unable to take the pity. "Had a whole bunch of tests, and one of the scans found the tumor. About the size of a grape at that point. 'Probably benign,' they said. The doctors were hoping they could keep me stable with some non-invasive options, so they put me on anti-seizure meds—and a mess of others."

If we're going to spend any significant amount of time together, she has to know what she could be dealing with. "Grab my jeans?"

Inara reaches for the crumpled denim next to her.

I fish the pill case out of my pocket, then open the lid. "If I start to slur my words more than usual or can't walk a straight line, I need one of the white pills. I can usually feel a seizure coming, and I'll warn you. But I can be non-verbal for anywhere from five minutes to half an hour."

"And the yellow pills?" She cups my hand, her tone all business, and I relax a little.

"Vertigo. I haven't needed one in a month, and I don't think I'll ever need them again. But I carry them just in case."

"One white pill if you slur your words or can't walk a straight line," she says, and I nod. "What about calling 911? Getting you to the hospital?"

"That shouldn't be necessary—"

She cuts me off with a searing kiss, then pulls back, pinning me with her stare. "We're soldiers, Royce. We prepare for the worst. And...I think we could have something here. This isn't the last night I plan to spend with you."

I could lose myself in her eyes. Her scent. The feel of her hands on my skin. "Emergency inst-sstructions are in my wallet, taped to the back of my driver's license. But only call if I pass out or if I'm not better in half an hour. Even when I can't speak, I can understand you, and I can give you non-verbal responses."

"Okay." She relaxes against me once more, and we stare out the window overlooking Lake Washington. "So, you didn't date because you were worried how a woman would react to you having a seizure?"

I love this view. And it's so much better having someone to share it with. "That was only part of it. I tried—once or twice—after I started on meds, but I was nauseous all the time and pretty fucking angry. Once I reached the acceptance stage, I was too sick. Kind of hard to date when you can't stay up later than 9:00 p.m."

"And now?" She presses closer, and if she didn't feel so damn good against me, I'd carry her to my bed right now.

"Eighty-five, ninety percent." The lump in my throat tightens my voice. "My balance sucks. As the night goes on, my speech will probably get slower. I'll stutter a little. If I get overtired, I can have clusters of seizures for a couple of days. This is...my life now. My doctors think I'm about as good as I'm going to get. Doesn't mean I won't keep trying for better, but this is who I am."

After a long moment, Inara flashes me a wicked grin, then tosses my jeans at me. "Come on, soldier. Get dressed. The woman *I* am now is hungry. And then after that, we're going to see about round two. And maybe," she leans in, crushes her mouth to mine, and pulls away with a quick bite to my lower lip, "I'll get to see what you look like tied to your bed."

I grab her, one arm around her waist and my other hand in her hair, fisting the short strands. "We'll see who ends up restrained."

"One of my college roommates was Italian," I say as I serve Inara a second helping of puttanesca. "From Boston. He taught me his favorite recipes. Without Damian, I probably would have starved."

"I *technically* know how to cook," Inara replies. "But takeout is a lot easier. And this is delicious."

"Not too spicy?" I arch a brow, unable to tear my gaze away from how her breasts swell against the Henley. As sexy as her golden tank was, seeing her comfortable, relaxed, in my home—and my shirt—was well worth digging out an old gray army t-shirt to finish out the vertical portion of the evening.

"I won a challenge in basic training by eating a whole ghost pepper. Without breaking a sweat," she teases with a smile. "Damn thing tasted like shit, but everyone else ended up throwing up or running for the milk to quell the burn. Can't say I had a pleasant time the next day, but the bragging rights were worth it."

Dinner passes with the conversation flowing easily. Her work as a translator, her last trip to England to see her father's family, and finally, my history with Emerald City Security.

"After I retired from the army, I bounced around for a while. Spent a couple of years in Silicon Valley, but the whole start-up culture? I'm too old for that shit."

"How'd you end up in Seattle?" Inara sits back and takes a sip of her wine.

"I like the weather."

"Bullshit." She laughs and runs a hand through her hair.

The other reason I haven't dated? Discussions like this. How do you tell a woman you've just fucked—no, scratch that—a woman you've just come damn close to making love to that you moved up here for someone else? Someone she knows? But as Inara leans forward, her sweet scent surrounding me, I don't want to hide anything from her.

"I don't have a lot of close friends," I say as I rise and pick up our plates. "Cam became sort of a sister when we were deployed together. Her family cut her off before she enlisted, and when you're diffusing bombs for a living...you get really fucking close really fucking fast."

She follows me into the kitchen with the pasta bowl. "I get it. Pretty sure my guys knew my entire life story two weeks after we deployed."

Leaning against the counter, I wrap my arm around Inara's waist and tug her closer. "After Cam got blown up, I bolted." With a sigh, I tip my head back to stare at the ceiling. "Not my finest hour. I moved to Seattle to try to make things right."

"Well, it must have worked." Inara cups my cheek, a smile curving her full lips. "Or we never would have met."

"Eventually." I tap the side of my head. "One of the few good things to come from the tumor. Reconnecting with one of my closest friends, my app...and you."

After a kiss that leaves me hard as a rock, Inara reaches up to slide her fingers into my short, cropped hair. "Show me this fabulous app you're building. And then I want you naked."

8

Inara

Royce leads me into a small bedroom he's turned into an office. Electronic parts litter a long table, and lines of code scroll by on a large monitor.

"What's all this?" I pick up a small, black piece of plastic the size of my thumb. A thin cable connects it to the computer, and a single light flickers on the side. Red, then green, then red again.

Royce taps the keyboard, and another screen appears with a flashing blue dot on a map of Seattle—right about where we are. "That little transmitter gave me a purpose when I was barely able to function." Pride swells his chest slightly. "When I started tinkering with app programming, I just needed a distraction. I couldn't walk, could barely use my left hand. But my mind worked. Cam would drive me to therapy, and I'd be so beaten up by the time I got home again that I'd end up trapped on my couch or in bed for hours. After I blew through two hundred hours of Band of Brothers and all of the Ken Burns documentaries, I started tinkering."

He runs a hand through his hair, and the move highlights his corded muscles.

Royce goes over the basics of the app with me. All of the tracking functions, the emergency beacon, the admin controls, and his future plans. "I can get biometrics from some of the more advanced smartwatches on the market today. So why not let caregivers check on their charges? 'Uncle Bob hasn't moved for the past three hours. Send him a message and make sure he hasn't fallen and can't get up. Or send the EMTs right to his location.' I'll give Cam a full license to sell the software as part of Oversight, but I think this could be huge. And I have a couple of other app ideas to play with once I've finished Loc8tion."

"How come you're not doing all of this for Emerald City?"

His blue eyes darken, the metallic streaks disappearing into cobalt. "Because I still have days I probably shouldn't get out of bed. I can't let the rest of the team down when my body decides I'm going to have a seizure cluster. Or when I'm meeting with a client and lose my words." He tucks his chin on top of my head as we stare at the screen showing some of Loc8tion's admin functions—directing the police right to a user's location, sending a loud alarm to the device to alert people around them, and displaying all the places a user has been in the past twenty-four hours. "Cam's worked too hard to have me ruin things for her. She deserves Emerald City all to herself."

"You wouldn't 'ruin things,' Royce." I turn in his arms, peering up at him. "I don't know Cam that well. But West and I tend to stick together on missions—there's an odd closeness you develop when you have to stop someone from bleeding out while bouncing over jungle roads in the middle of fucking nowhere. But from what little he and I have talked about Cam and Emerald City, you 'ruining things' isn't a concern."

"Oh, I can ruin things with the best of them," he says, almost too quietly for me to hear.

"What?"

With a sigh, he shakes his head. "Cam and I are working our way back to solid. But with what I did to her...it's a long road. And I don't want to fuck it up."

"What does that mean?" I cringe at my bluntness, but I suck at the "getting to know you" portion of the dating game—always have.

"I was her CO when she was blown up. Hell, I was only a couple hundred feet away." He leads me back to the couch, his shoulders slumping, his gait a little more uneven than usual. "I should have seen the other bombs. Should have listened to Yanko when he warned me something wasn't right. I hesitated. And in that second...she ss-stepped on a trigger plate. Didn't have a fucking chance." He clenches his fists as he stares into the flames of the small gas fireplace along the wall.

The whole story spills out as he rests his elbows on his knees. "The insurgents liked to set traps for our ordinance teams. Bombs on top of bombs. Daisy-chained sets of explosives hidden under piles of rubble. Cam had just finished diffusing the primary bomb—the only one we saw. One of my guys warned me. Or tried to. I cut him off because hell, she was almossst done. She stood up, turned, and froze. Those three seconds are burned into my brain. The horror. The fear. Fuck." Royce shakes his head, and I run my hand down his back. "She knew she was dead. Or close to it. The explosions threw her thirty feet. By the time I got to her, the arm of her sssuit had started to melt, and she was close to bleeding out from a piece of pipe that had torn clean through her side."

"Shit."

Royce meets my gaze, and the pain etched on his face threatens to make my eyes burn. "Once we reached the field hospital...I left. Didn't see her again for almost three years. I kept tabs...through the other guys in the unit, but she asked about me every damn day. I failed her once. I won't do it again. I'll maintain a small stake in Emerald City, but it's Cam's company now. Or will be by next week. Shhe and I are meeting with my l-lawyer on T-Tuesday."

"Royce?"

The marked change in Royce's stutter makes my heart beat faster, and he blows out a breath. "Sorry. This happens at n-night. I'm fine. N-nothing to worry about."

I cup his cheeks and search his gaze. He's not concerned. Hurt. Tired. But not the least bit afraid. In this position, pressed against him, I can sense his heartbeat. Calm, steady. "This is all new to me."

"Being with someone...d-damaged?" The right side of his mouth lifts a little higher than the left.

"Being with someone. Period." I lean in for a kiss, and the taste of him makes me want more—much more. All of him. Straddling his thighs, I slide my hands into his hair. "I don't get close to people, Royce. I've dated. Had a few semi-serious flings. But every time I go out on a job with Ryker, there's a chance I won't come back."

"You forget what I used to do for a living, baby. I underst-sstand. Live in the moment. You never know when you might die —or have a st-stroke and wind up unable to walk or talk." Royce stands, pulls me to my feet, and cups my ass. "I'm done wasting t-time."

"Me too." Kissing my way from his lips to his ear, I drop my voice. "I want you naked."

His arousal juts against my bruised hip, but I stifle my wince as he cups my ass and lifts me against him. "Oh, do you?" Now, a gruff edge replaces the wistful tone, and his dark blue eyes shine with silver flecks as he carries me down the hall to his bedroom.

"Yes." I close my teeth over the shell of his ear, and I'm rewarded with a shudder and his fingers digging into my butt cheeks as he carries me down the hall.

Once we reach his bedroom, Royce claims my mouth in a kiss

that can only be described as panty-melting, and I grind my hips against him. "Take me, soldier."

Despite the desperation in his kiss, he's gentle as he sets me down on the bed. "Do you trust me?"

"Yes."

He slides a drawer open and withdraws a set of padded leather cuffs. "Enough to let me tie you up?"

"Enough for anything."

"Fuck, Royce. I'm going to come...again!" On my back, with my legs wrapped around his waist, I can't stop the release barreling towards me. Have we been at this minutes? Or hours? Time means nothing, and even my voice deserts me as I implode, my back arching as the seemingly endless waves of pleasure roll through me.

He groans his climax, and despite the condom, I feel every-thing...every pulse of his cock inside me, every brush of his fingers, the way the light dusting of hair on his chest tickles my breasts, his trembling abs as he holds himself over me.

"You...are...going t-to kill me," he says with something between a smile and a grimace as he releases my wrists from the leather cuffs, then pulls out of me and stumbles to the bathroom to dispose of the condom.

In a few moments, he's back, but strain tightens lines around his eyes and mouth.

"Are you okay?" Despite feeling like my bones are made of wet noodles and my brain has taken a permanent vacation, I push up on an elbow and reach out to cup his cheek.

He nods as he slides under the sheets and urges me to snuggle close. With a wry half-smile, he gestures to the clock.

"Oh God. How is it 2:00 a.m.?"

"You're d-delicious. That'sss how." His speech is decidedly slurred now, and I cup his cheek as a frustrated half-growl escapes his lips. "Tired."

"Is this normal or do I need to worry?"

With a tender, lingering kiss, he settles my nerves, though his eyes are only half open and I'm pretty sure he's already mostly asleep when his head hits the pillow once more. "N-normal. Jussst need rest, baby."

"I'm going to clean up a little. Get a glass of water, okay?"

He doesn't answer me, his soft breaths against my cheek reassuring. Slowly easing myself out of his embrace, I take a moment to stare at him.

Stretched out on his side, the moonlight slanting in from high windows paint his face in a gentle glow. I lost count of the number of times he made me come, but we were approaching double digits.

My ass stings as I scoot off the bed. Turns out we're both a fan of a good spanking, and I smooth my hand along my overheated skin. "Best night ever, soldier," I whisper as I lean down to brush a kiss behind his ear, right along the scar leftover from his surgery.

Once I've washed my face and made use of the travel toothbrush I threw in my bag at the last minute, I pad out to the kitchen, wearing nothing but Royce's shirt.

As I grab a glass from the cabinet, a shadow moves outside the kitchen window.

What the hell?

I brace my hands against the sink to try to get a better view. A man dressed in a hoodie and carrying a small backpack ambles down the alley. At least we'd turned off the kitchen light, so he probably couldn't see my little half-naked shuffle.

An odd sensation prickles along the back of my neck, and I fill the glass as I watch him turn the corner. It's an alley for fuck's sake. Not private property. The trash cans are back there, along with a handful of parking spaces.

Get a grip. And get back to bed.

Royce is exactly where I left him, and as I snuggle close to his side, he wraps an arm around me. "Missed...you," he mumbles before he falls asleep again.

I'm in trouble. Two dates and ten days, and I think I'm already starting to fall in love with this man.

9

Royce

I HAVEN'T FELT this damn good since before the tumor, and we stayed up past 2:00 a.m. "After breakfast," I say as I wrap my arms around Inara's waist from behind and brush a kiss to the back of her neck, "want to go up to Snoqualmie to see the falls?"

"I have a better idea. Breakfast at the lodge overlooking the falls. Or...lunch, at least." Her cheeks flush, though her bronzed skin hides most of the embarrassment. She tips her head so I can claim her lips, and damn, I can't get enough of her taste. Gently twisting her in my arms so we're face to face, I slide my hands down to cup her ass.

She purrs, and the corners of my lips tug into a grin as I pull away. "Great idea. But next time, we're hitting this little diner on the corner of Broadway and Pike."

"And when would this 'next time' be?" Inara wriggles out of my arms, then darts around the kitchen counter to grab her purse. "Next Saturday morning?"

I make a show of checking my phone, but it's not like I have anything else taking up my nights. "I can probably squeeze you in."

A dish towel sails towards me, and I snatch the cloth from the air just before it hits me in the face. "Oh, now I'm going to do more than squeeze you in," I say as I stalk over to her. Her eyes widen as I pin her arms behind her back. Pressing against her, I let her feel my growing erection, and she shudders in my grasp. "And I'm not waiting a week to see you again. How about tomorrow night?"

Inara's smile dims, a storm gathering in her gray eyes. "I wish. I'm taking West and the new guy out to Wenatchee tomorrow for long-range target practice. Then Ryker wants us all running drills on Monday night."

"Tuesday, then?" Threading my fingers through her hair, I cup the back of her head and slant a gentle kiss over her lips.

"It's a date."

If we don't get out of here soon, she's going to end up naked again—not that I'd mind. But her stomach rumbles, and we both laugh. "Your place or mine?"

"I'll sleep anywhere—as long as you're next to me. You make me feel...safe."

Something in her voice speaks of a deep longing, and I cup her cheek, tracing my thumb over the smooth skin. "You don't normally feel safe? Now I'm worried."

Inara tries to look away, down at the counter, but I nudge her chin up until she meets my gaze. Sadness swims in her eyes, along with another emotion I can't identify. "Talk to me, baby. We just...fuck. That was one of the most intense nights of my life, and it was only our third date. We're either building something here, or we're going to explode and burn out in a week." I seal my declaration with a tender kiss. "I know which I'd prefer."

Extracting herself from my arms, she leans against the opposite wall of my kitchen, her hands clasped together, fingers twisting. "I'm not good at the whole 'opening up' part of relationships."

"I'm not asking for your deepest, darkest secrets. Unless you buried DB Cooper in your backyard. That might be good to know." I crack a smile, but instead of joining me in the joke, Inara stifles a wince. I take a step towards her, but the look in her eyes stops me. "Inara?"

Her eyes shine in the morning sunlight streaming through the window. "Coop...Cooper," she whispers, "died in Columbia."

Oh fuck. Joking about a long-missing, legendary airplane robber should have been a safe subject, but I've touched a nerve with the name. Not that I know who "Coop" is or when Inara was in Columbia. "Can I hold you?"

Even the safest question I can think of doesn't bring her back to me. Instead, she scoots out of the kitchen and heads for the bathroom. The door shuts before I can move, and I curse my lousy sense of humor, my timing, my overwhelming desire to get to know this woman. Now I don't know what to do. Go after her? Or give her some space? Either option could lead to disaster. This is why guys fuck up so much. We're not as dumb as we seem—we just can't make a decision to save our lives where women are concerned.

Fuck it. She's upset, and I caused it. I've got to fix it.

Before I reach the bathroom door, she emerges, and it's like she's slid a mask back in place. Her eyes are clear, her lip no longer quivers, and her jaw juts out slightly in challenge. "I'm sorry," she says, just a little too brightly. "Bad memories."

"Who was he?"

Confusion shifts the mask slightly, but not enough for me to see the real Inara underneath. "Cam never told you what happened when West got shot?"

I search my memories. "Oh, shit. She never said his name. I'm so sorry, baby. I didn't know." Reaching for her, I'm relieved when she doesn't pull away, but she doesn't relax into my embrace either. "Were you close?"

The scent of my shampoo in her hair fills my nose as her head tucks under my chin, and I can't get enough of her. I trace circles on her back with my palm, and eventually, she melts against me as I lead her to the couch and sink down with her.

"No. Not really. He was...kind of an ass. Disobeyed orders all the time. Ryker was going to let him go as soon as he found a replacement. But he didn't deserve to die." Her breath heaves, and she tightens her hold on me. "I...I should have been faster. Maybe then..." After a single shudder, she stills, and before I can offer any more words of comfort, she swallows hard. "I'd need a lot more alcohol for the rest of this conversation." Desperation darkens the storm in her eyes. "Another time, okay?"

There isn't a single thing I'd refuse this woman—not with the pain swirling in her gaze and her jaw clenched like she's keeping herself together by sheer force of will.

"Okay. But...I'm going to hold you to that, eventually. Doesn't have to be soon, but..." Am I wrong? Fear takes hold. "We *are* building something here, aren't we? I've never wanted to know anyone as intimately as I want to know you."

Inara's lips curve into a weak grin. "We are, Royce. Just...give me a little time."

"Fuck." Another transmitter tumbles from my unsteady fingers. The soldering iron hisses as I drop it onto my desk, and I curse again, yanking the plug from the wall and setting the iron to rights. I flex my hand, articulate each finger one at a time as if playing scales on the piano. My eyes burn, and the all-too-familiar tingles at the base of my skull warn me I need to take my meds if I want to avoid a seizure. Inara and I had only intended to spend half of yesterday together, but we'd ended the night as we'd started the morning—in my bed. Around 3:00 a.m., Inara kissed me softly, apologized, and slipped out the door where West was waiting to take her and the new guy over the mountains.

My phone vibrates on the corner of the desk.

Made it here safely. Can't wait until Tuesday. Got a working transmitter yet?

I should probably be honest. It's not like I can hide the effects of the stroke. If we're really building something here—and hell, I'm half in love with her already—she's going to see me at my worst. But she's also three hours away, and I don't want her to worry. I opt for a half-truth, hoping she won't push me for more.

Hands aren't steady today, so it's slow going. About to head to yoga. Should be able to finish up afterward.

That's not a lie. But just because I *should* be able to finish, doesn't mean my body will cooperate.

"One more try." Stubbornness is a great quality during recovery. Not so much today.

Gently closing the transmitter in my tiny vise, I blow out a deep breath and start the soldering iron again. This time, I line the pins up perfectly with my right hand, and with my damaged left, pick up the tool and say a quick prayer. "Work, dammit."

Five minutes later, tiny dots of metal mar the desk, but once I plug the transmitter into my computer, lines of code stream by. "Hooah," I say as I pump my fist. Some days, the little wins aren't enough. Being able to calm my tremors, stave off a seizure, or walk a straight line are great accomplishments, but I want more.

Today...I miss the old Royce. And despite Inara's preference for new Royce, I can't help longing for who I used to be. Or at least...what I used to be able to do.

Grabbing the transmitter, I toss it into my bag with my wallet and keys before washing down my meds with the last of my luke-warm coffee. Maybe today's the day I finally master Crow pose.

Inara

As West raps on my door, I sling my bag over my shoulder, then wince as it bangs against my hip.

"Hey, thanks for picking me up." I offer him a pained smile as I lock up.

"Thought you got your car back?"

Once I've climbed into the cab of his truck, I blow out a breath. "I did. But a friend just found out her mom's in the hospital. Eighty-three years old with a broken hip. So I lent her my car. And you know Ryker would give me shit for weeks if I ever took a Lyft to and from the warehouse."

West chuckles. "I'd pay to see that."

"Yeah, well, you wouldn't be his target. I might not survive the storm."

As he navigates the slick streets—a late winter snowstorm took everyone by surprise last night—I watch his face. "You're in a good mood."

His slanted look tells me I could have phrased that better, and I cringe. "Sorry. Just...shit. You're practically beaming, and we're going to get our asses kicked tonight. Spill. What happened?"

At a stoplight, West digs in his pocket. The small, square box arcs through the cab, and as I catch it, I know exactly what I'll find inside. "You're really going to do it."

Inside, a delicate silver filigree band holds five rubies. A second, thinner ring, is designed to fuse to the first. "Oh, West. She's going to love it."

"I hope so. After Uzbekistan, she agreed to move in with me. Hell, she brought it up. I've been asking her for months, but something about me being gone..." He runs a hand through his hair. "She's the least needy person I've ever met." With a grin, he jerks his head towards me, "Other than you. But something changed while we were gone."

"So...when are you going to ask her?"

"Haven't figured that part out yet. The way I feel, it'll be a miracle if I don't ask her the minute I get home tonight." He's practically giddy, and I hand the box back to him then offer a friendly punch to the shoulder.

"I'm happy for you. But you know Ryker's going to—"

"Yeah. So...keep this between us?" He shoves the ring back into the pocket of his jeans and meets my gaze as he parks outside the warehouse.

"Absolutely. But you're going to have to find a way to hide that smile. Ryker's no idiot. And you usually have a better poker face." I should know. I've lost to West every fucking time we've played cards.

"Somehow, I think once we get inside, that won't be a problem." West gestures to the warehouse door where Ryker stands with his arms folded across his chest.

Shit. We're five minutes late.

"Probably not. I'll fall on the sword. Hang back locking up the truck. Once he starts yelling at me, you shouldn't have a problem looking properly chastised." Hopping down with my bag, I ignore the lingering soreness from my brush with the electrical box and stride towards my doom.

"We've got another job," Ryker says as I approach. "And you're late."

"Um, snow?" I gesture to the piles of white fluffy stuff Seattle is so unused to. "When do we leave?"

"In an hour. Call in your excuses at the office and gear up." Our fearless leader's voice holds an unusual strain, and as I slip past him into the warehouse, I notice how bloodshot his eyes are.

"Ry?" I touch his arm. "What's different about this one?"

He holds my gaze as if needing a tether to his own sanity. But after a breath, he shakes off whatever personal horror has him in its grip. "I'll explain once we're airborne."

10

Royce

A LITTLE AFTER SIX, I walk into Libations. Cam waves from a back table—not far from the one Inara and I shared just a week ago.

We embrace, and when I pull back, Cam smiles as she sinks into her chair. "I wish you'd come to the office," she says. "You should see the new job board Orion set up. It's like something out of a techno-thriller. And everyone misses you."

"Maybe next week." I don't want to see it—don't want to see what she's done—changed. Yet, the papers in my bag give her the power to change anything she wants. After all, by the end of the night, the company will be hers.

I order a martini, three olives, to go with Cam's manhattan. After a bit of small talk—mostly about Loc8tion—I take the envelope from my bag and slide it across the table. Lifting my glass, I wait for her to return the gesture.

"Cam, you've done amazing things with Emerald City the past three months. Hell, you've accomplished everything I ever wanted for the company and more. In such a short time. I…"

Swallowing hard, I push the envelope closer to her. "Sign these, and Emerald City's yours. For good. You deserve it."

Her eyes darken, her lower lip askew as she chews on the inside of her cheek. "Royce...the tumor...?"

Whatever she heard in my voice brings a shine to those brown eyes, and I set my drink down as I realize what I've done. Reaching across the table, I grip her fingers. They're cool, the scar along the edge of her hand thick under my thumb. "Nothing's wrong, Cam. I swear. I just..." I shrug. "The work I'm doing with Loc8tion? I fucking love it. Once I release it, I have four more ideas lined up—all apps designed for people with memory issues, mobility problems, the elderly... I even have a game idea Manny said would be great for his rehab patients."

"And you don't love running Emerald City." Her voice lowers, flattens. "I always thought...you'd come back. But you're leaving...again."

The tear that tumbles down her cheek shocks me. "You've been kicking ass running things. You don't need me."

Cam flinches. "I've got to go." She turns and digs through her briefcase, coming away with a twenty, a pen, and a tissue that she swipes under her eyes. Ripping the envelope as she fights to remove the papers, she bites her lip so hard, I'm worried she's going to draw blood. But when I try to take her hand again, she flinches and pulls away.

Three signatures later, she shoves the paperwork and the twenty across the table, then reaches for her cane.

"Cam, what did I say?"

"Nothing. I just...can't do this with you again. I thought—I guess I was wrong."

She tries to get up, but in her haste, she doesn't notice the end of her cane resting on the flap of her messenger bag. As she skids, I catch her in my arms, and she breaks, silent sobs wracking her thin frame.

"Pint. Shit." Once I ease her back down, I slide my chair closer. "I thought you'd be happy about this."

She drags the back of her hand across her cheek, sniffles once, and reaches for her glass. Downing the manhattan in two vicious gulps, she meets my gaze, the fire in her eyes enough to make me wish for my bomb suit.

"Do you know why I took the job when you showed up at my door all those years ago?" Her injured hand spasms and the rocks glass clatters against the wood table. After I shake my head, she huffs. "I thought it was the only way I'd ever get my best friend back. If we worked together, you couldn't ignore me. Couldn't pretend I didn't exist anymore. But...I was wrong. Four years, and all we did was dance around the chasm between us. Until you told me about the tumor. You...came back."

"I was an ass. I'll apologize every d-day—" *Fuck. I won't. Because I won't be* there *every day.* I scrub my hands over my face, wishing the earth would open up and swallow me whole.

When I raise my head, I signal the bartender for two more drinks. Cam glares at me, but now, instead of fire, ice frosts her gaze. We don't speak until the drinks arrive, and Cam thanks the bartender by name.

"You all right, darlin'?" Garrett asks, not even sparing me a glance.

"Fine. Long day. When are you and Lilah going to come over for dinner again?"

"Name the day—well, as long as it's not a weekend. Lilah has this new cheesecake recipe she wants to try out on unsuspecting victims—err, friends."

Cam chuckles. "Better her cooking than mine. Call West. Set something up."

"You got it, darlin'."

Alone again with our drinks, I wait for Cam to take a healthy sip of her manhattan. "Pint, I know there's still an ocean of shit we have to swim through before we're...where we want to be. I hurt you. In ways I'll probably never understand. But I'm not *going* anywhere. I just won't be in the office every day."

She blinks back the tears glistening in her eyes. "I used to come into work early because I figured you'd have to at least say 'good morning.' I thought when you came back...fuck. I don't know. I miss working with you, Royce."

With her every word, guilt crushes me further. I scrub my hands over my face, wishing I could take back the past ten years. I should have stayed after the bombs. Gone to see her. Called her. Anything other than disappearing when she needed me the most.

The lump in my throat makes it hard to speak. "We made a good team."

"Yeah."

Taking a chance, I nudge the paperwork towards her. "Did you even read these?"

She scans the first page. "Standard transfer of ownership."

"Keep reading." I slide one of the olives off the toothpick, watching for the moment she understands.

Cam's eyes widen. "You're licensing Loc8tion to Emerald City?"

"Yes. For five percent of the residuals for three years, you get an unlimited license, and I get to spend my time developing additional apps. And consult whenever you deploy Loc8tion."

"But..."

"Cam—" I reach across the table again, but this time she lets me link our fingers. "With me in charge, we're going to fall back into old patterns. But it'll be worse. I'll work too hard, wind up flat on my back for a week, then you'll have to cover for me. Doing your job and mine. That's not good for either of us. This way...we get to start over. As friends. No boss/employee shit to get in the way. And I'll be around whenever you deploy Loc8tion."

"Oh." She's still not convinced, but the pain in her eyes fades, and she tries for a smile—almost succeeding. "I can't lose you, Royce. You and West and Lucas are the only family I have."

I lift my martini, trying again for the toast she refused me the last time. "You're not going to lose me, Pint. I promise."

Cam's phone buzzes, and a moment later, mine follows. My heart skips a beat as we answer two separate calls.

"What's wrong?" I ask.

Inara sighs from the other end of the line. "We caught a job. Last minute. I don't know what it is or when we'll be back. But Ryker's—" she lowers her voice, "—not himself."

"Do I need to worry?" I risk a glance at Cam, and her bronzed skin has gone pale. I turn away from her and cup my hand over the receiver. "I'm having drinks with Cam."

"All I know is that it's a standard K&R job. As soon as we're back, I'll call. But, I might not make our date tomorrow night." A male voice I don't recognize calls her name, and she curses under her breath. "I gotta go. I...I'll miss you, Royce."

I want to say something more than 'I'll miss you, too.' But not over the phone. "Come back safe, baby. Call me as soon as you can."

When I hang up and turn back to Cam, she's staring down at her phone. "He'll be fine," I say.

Cam meets my gaze, and a knowing smile curves her lips. "So will she."

Inara

A little after eight, sitting in the belly of a C140 transport plane headed for a tiny town in Mexico, West, Graham, and I wait for Ryker to explain the last-minute, high-priority job. The new guy whined about canceling a date with his girl, and Ryker hasn't forgiven him yet, so Graham doesn't earn more than a quick glance as Ryker rubs a hand over his bald head.

"The target is my CO's kid. My...godson." Though he can't whisper—even with our headsets on, the roar of the engines forces us to yell—the edge to his voice says he can't quite believe he's headed off to rescue someone he knows.

"Where, when, and how?" West asks.

Good. Cut right to the heart of the matter. Keep Ryker occupied with the mission, and maybe his emotions will stay firmly where he keeps them every other day of his life.

"A compound outside of Guadalajara. Ty's with Doctors Without Borders. The earthquake last week? Decimated a handful of poor villages north of Durango. We don't know much. Dozer—my CO—got the ransom demand a few hours ago. Four million."

"Shit. For a doctor? Why do they think they can get that much for him?" As Ryker pins me with a hard glare, I hold up my hands. "That's not a judgment on who he is as a person, Ry. But... that's a sum only HVTs go for."

"He's not a high-value target. Not that I know of. But Dozer bought Amazon and Apple stock when they were cheap. Anyone who searches Ty's name can figure out his net worth. But that's beside the point. They've only given Dozer until 9:00 a.m. tomorrow, or they're going to kill Ty. We have to figure out an infil and exfil plan in the next four hours if we have any chance of getting him out before dawn."

West pulls out his tablet. "Coordinates?"

Rattling off the GPS codes for latitude and longitude like he's reciting his own phone number, Ryker stares past us, as if he can see through the fuselage out into the darkening sky.

Royce

By the end of the night, we're both a little less than sober. After two drinks, we split a Lyft to her place—well, her and West's place—where she poured us generous shots of bourbon.

"I lived alone for six years," she says as she swirls the caramel-colored liquid in her glass. "And now, I hate being here without him. What's wrong with me?"

"You're in love? Pretty sure that's what's supposed t-to happen." The bourbon burns a trail down my throat, and I sink back against the overstuffed couch cushions. "When did you know?"

Her head swivels towards me, her mouth forming a little *o*. "You're falling for Inara."

I reach into my pocket for a small pouch. My fingers fumble with the drawstring, and I let the necklace spill into Cam's palm. "I wandered through Pike Place earlier today. Is it too soon for jewelry?"

Cam lets the silver chain dangle from her fingers. The kunzite pendant, a pink teardrop that the vendor told me would protect the wearer from emotional turmoil, takes on a subtle shine.

"If West had given me this after two weeks together, I would have bolted." She runs her thumb over the stone. "But Inara doesn't have my particular...damage."

"You're not—"

"I am." The bourbon sloshes in her glass as she sets it on the end table with more force than necessary. "I pushed him away when I needed him most. I could have lost him—forever—because I couldn't trust that someone could love me."

A fresh tear trails down her cheek, and I wrap my arm around her shoulders. "I had a hand in that." With a sigh, I rest my cheek against the top of her head. "All I saw, every time I closed my eyes, was your face in the moment before the bombs went off. You knew. For a split second before the first blast...you knew."

"I don't remember anything after I stood up," she says, her voice slurred from the bourbon. "Just you begging me to hold on. The scent of my skin burning. Blood."

"Cam—"

"Let me finish." Easing out from under my arm, she slides back on the couch, wincing as she draws her knees up. "I knew I was dead. I could feel it. The cold. The darkness. Hell, I might have even seen that tunnel with the light everyone talks about. But I didn't want to disappoint you. My surrogate big brother. My best friend. You were the only person in my life who *knew* me. The real me. Hell, even Yanko didn't know my secrets. I lived because of you."

"And that's why I disappeared on you." I reach for my glass, needing the liquid courage to finish out this conversation. "My brother and I can't spend more than two hours together without tearing each other apart. Our mother died fifteen years ago. Dad not long after that. I joined the army to find a new family. Then this whip-smart pint-sized ordnance specialist joined my team. You swore like a sailor, followed every single order—some of them with a whole lot of cursing—and walked up to your first bomb like it was a piece of candy."

She finishes off the bottle, and I'm already regretting the hangover I'm going to have in the morning. But the chasm between us is shrinking by the minute, and while I worry she'll kick me out when I'm done, I need to finish it.

"I spent a week drunk off my ass. I was sure you were going to blame me, and I couldn't look into your eyes and *not* see that total and complete trust you had in me. I asked for reassignment so I could start over."

"Did it work?" She peers up at me, her eyes bloodshot.

"No." I finish off my drink, then pull out my phone to call a Lyft to bring me home. "But starting over now...that has promise."

Inara

Through my scope, I watch Graham and West take out the two guards at the east corner of the compound's terra-cotta-colored wall. "All clear," West says over comms and laces his hands together so he can give Graham a boost over the wall.

The kid scrambles up and over, dropping down behind a large banyan tree. A rope sails back over the wall and the former SEAL joins Graham a few seconds later.

"Shift change in five minutes," Ryker mutters as he starts the Hummer three hundred yards from the front gates.

West taps his earbud. "Hostiles." Three silenced shots ring out—darts designed to render a two-hundred-pound man unconscious for an hour. As West updates us, "Breaching front door," I let out the breath I didn't know I'd been holding.

I can picture the two of them—West down on one knee, picking the lock with a speed no other human can match, and Graham on alert, his weapon ready, hazel eyes scanning for more hostiles.

"Four minutes. Get your asses moving," Ryker snaps.

I roll my eyes. "Calm down. This isn't our first mission. You want to turn this into a bloodbath?"

"I want Ty out of there."

Ryker would normally have my ass for challenging him on comms, but this job is anything but situation normal. "Ry, they'll get him."

"Hostiles neutralized. Target secure. Coming out. Three on foot," West says, and I angle my rifle towards the east side of the compound, slowing my heart rate, controlling my breathing, and narrowing my focus to the path I know they'll take.

Graham passes through my sights first, followed by a tired, bedraggled-looking young man with a black eye and his left arm cradled against his stomach. West brings up the rear, side-stepping so he can keep an eye on their six.

They reach the wall, and West and Graham swap positions. "Hold on to me," West says, and Ty puts his arm around West's neck, letting the SEAL carry him up and over the wall. Graham scrambles after them, and when they're all running towards Ryker and the Hummer, I grab my rifle and gear and head for the rendezvous point.

"Can't ask for a better mission." I clap Ryker on the shoulder once we're in the air on the way home. Ty's asleep, his dislocated shoulder back in its socket and a sling holding his arm immobile. Ryker hugged the kid when we got onto the plane, and I swear I saw tears in his eyes.

"He never should have been in danger." Ryker shoves his hands into his pockets as he sinks down onto one of the benches that line the fuselage. "I don't know why they took him. Neither does he."

"Sometimes it's just a crime of opportunity," I offer as I unwrap a protein bar. Offering Ryker half, I shrug when he refuses. "Your loss. These are a lot better than those MREs you pack."

"It doesn't make any sense."

"What doesn't?" West joins us, and unlike our prickly leader, accepts the offered piece of peanut butter and chia bar with a nod.

"Got any more of those?" Graham asks. "I've had enough 'chocolate brownie surprise' to last a lifetime."

With a chuckle, West snatches the MRE from our newest team member. "I'll take that. Cam's got some weird fascination with these things. Says they taste just like her grandmother's brownies."

"Sounds like you're lucky you never had to endure her grandmother's cooking." I toss Graham another protein bar, digging my third—and final—precious treat from my stash.

"Ask Royce to tell you how many times Cam beat him at poker—and how many times she refused his money, but took her payment in brownies," West says, and my heart flips a little. I'd very much like to ask Royce a lot of things right now. To kiss me, to tear these fatigues off me, to make use of the new leather cuffs I bought on Etsy that should be sitting in my mailbox right now...

"Earth to Ry." West reaches over and gives Ryker's shoulder a squeeze. "You haven't been here all mission, man. The kid's safe. We got him out. He was in the wrong place at the wrong time. That's all."

Ryker scrubs his hands over his face. Scars cover almost every inch of him—except for his left cheek, left jawbone, and around his left eye. Burns, cuts, broken bones...the assholes who ran Hell tortured him within an inch of his life, let him heal up, and then did it again. Fifteen months he survived until someone made a mistake—underestimated him. He never told me the whole story, but his escape is the stuff of legends in the Rangers, Special Forces, and the SEALs. At least six of the guards died that day, the rest three weeks later when West and his team breached Hell and tore it apart.

Ryker takes a swig from his water bottle before returning his gaze to his boots. "Ty wasn't in a dangerous area. He's a rule

follower if there ever was one. He said...before he fell asleep...
that he heard one of them say they'd get paid either way."

"Either way?" I lean forward, unsure I heard him over the roar
of the engines.

"Yeah." Ryker empties the bottle, wipes his crooked mouth,
and stares at his godson. "There's more to this than bad luck."

11

Inara

WEST HAS his phone in his hand the second we reach his truck. He thumbs out a quick message to Cam, then squints in the harsh winter sunlight. "At least most of the snow melted."

"There's a bonus." I stifle a yawn. "She okay?"

"She's at work. And apparently...hung over." With a chuckle, West starts the engine. "After I drop you off, I'll head to her office. Kind of puts a damper on the whole 'proposal' plan, though. I'd prefer she not puke all over the ring."

"I should call Royce." Yet, I don't reach for my phone. As much as I want to be in his arms right now, or in his bed, something stops me. When we left Ryker, he warned us both to be careful, and I glance over at West. "You think there's anything to worry about?"

"You mean Ryker's vague 'watch your backs' talk?" West shakes his head. "Normally, I'd trust his instincts. The bastard found a way to break out of Hell. But he just had to hear his godson scream as we popped his shoulder back into the socket."

"What did they do to him?" Turning my phone over and over

again in my hands, I hear Coop scream in my memories for a split second before I force my guilt back into its locked box once more.

With a sigh, West merges onto the freeway. "The kid was beaten up, bound, gagged, and thrown into a dark basement. He held it together pretty well once we got outside, but you didn't see him when we found him. Ty practically started crying when Graham pulled the hood off his head and said we were there to help."

"Pretty standard reaction, yeah?"

Laying on the horn as a truck almost cuts us off, West curses under his breath before answering. "Textbook. But that's not my point. Fuck, I'm so tired I'm rambling. Ryker knows what happens to the targets we rescue. He spent fifteen hours with a hundred scenarios running through his head. Maybe more, after all he's been through." He pauses, then shoots me a quick glance. "There are only three people in this world I trust with my life. Cam, Ryker, and you. But right now, I won't take anything Ryker says at face value. Give him a couple of days to gain a little perspective. If he still feels the same way, then I'll worry."

Once I'm home, I call Royce, and his slurred speech makes my heart skip more than one beat until he launches FaceTime.

"Didn't ssleep well," he says as the right side of his mouth curves into a weak smile. "T-told you bad days surprise me ssome-t-times. Be fine t-tomorrow."

"No seizures?" I don't even know if I should ask, but this is all new territory for me—caring about someone with chronic health problems, hell, caring about someone period—and seeing the strong, proud man I'm falling for struggle to form words hurts me in ways I didn't expect.

"None. Jusst need resst. But tomorrow…"

I'm tempted to brush my fingers over the screen, but instead, I force a smile. "Tomorrow let me cook you dinner. Or maybe bring over some takeout."

"Youuu got it."

He disconnects the call a second before I say, "I miss you."

I can't sleep, so I opt for a blazing hot shower, half a pot of coffee, and some light work from my couch. One of the benefits of my day job? I can translate from anywhere.

Two press releases and a transfer of ownership document later, I wonder how Sonia's doing. Punching in her number, I frown when her voicemail picks up. She's always glued to her phone. "Hey, Sonia. I'm back in town. How's your mom? My car didn't give you any trouble, did she? Want me to bring a bottle of wine over tonight? Or some takeout? Give me a call." I should go to bed early, but I don't want to be alone.

The day passes with short naps, plodding translations, and more coffee. By the time the sun starts to dip towards the horizon, I'm so caffeinated I'm practically vibrating, and my stomach has turned sour.

Shit. I forgot to eat today. There's a great little Thai place a couple of blocks away, so I bundle up in my wool coat—it's still icy out with a few light flurries—and head for the dimly-lit restaurant.

As soon as I place my order for pad thai and fresh rolls, my phone buzzes with a text message.

Slept most of the day. Woke up missing you. If you're awake, call me. The aphasia's mostly gone.

I'm grinning like a damn fool when I dial his number. I don't know why, but I need connection right now.

"You're the best distraction," he purrs, his voice thick with sleep, but only slightly slurred.

"From what?"

"These fucking transmitters." A hint of strain colors Royce's words. "I need t-ten of them for Emerald City to test Loc8tion. But they're so d-damn delicate." He swears under his breath, then a quiet clatter carries over the line. "Fuck it. Thought I could manage the detail work for a few minutes, but I guess I was a little overly optimistic. How was your day off?"

"I don't do 'days off' very well. I worked from my couch. Drank way too much coffee." I accept the takeout bag and start the short walk home as the snow swirls around me.

"Can you talk about your trip?" Royce sighs, and I imagine him stretching out on his couch...then imagine us on that couch together, naked...until he clears his throat. "Inara?"

"Sorry. I was...um, wishing I was there right now."

"Where?"

"On top of you. Or...under you. Next to you. Anywhere in close proximity. Without any clothes on." Despite the chill in the air, I'm not cold as I unlock my front door and slip inside.

He releases a frustrated, deeply erotic groan. "Fuck. You don't know what you do to me, baby. I missed you last night."

"Missed you too. I was in a seedy motel outside of Guadalajara. Routine job. Except for the target. Ryker's godson. We couldn't find a single fucking reason why they'd take him—other than his father's money. But how would the cartel even know Ty was there?"

"Social media maybe? These days, even the smallest, most ass-backward terrorist groups have the internet. What's his name? I can run some searches on him, see if he posted anything publicly that might have put a target on his back."

"Tyler Goz. Ryker's convinced—"

My doorbell rings as I'm tearing open the takeout bag. "Hang on." As I check the peephole, my stomach flips. "Royce...I need to call you back." Not waiting for his reply, I shove the phone into my pocket as I pull the door open. "Can I help you?"

The young, uniformed police officer holds a small piece of paper in his hand. "Are you Inara Ruzgani?"

I zero in on his name tag. "May I see your badge, Officer Franklin?" His uniform looks perfect, but you can never be too careful.

While he waits, his badge held out so I can see, I make a quick call to the Seattle PD. They verify his identity, and as Royce texts me asking if I'm okay, I return my focus to the young man. "I'm Inara, yes. What's this about?"

"We're investigating a hit-and-run that happened late last night, Ms. Ruzgani. Involving your car and a Ms. Sonia Nolan. Ms. Nolan is in the hospital, but we recovered the registration from your vehicle."

"Oh my God." I stumble back, my voice cracking. "Is she going to be okay? What happened?"

"I can't share her condition, ma'am." Officer Franklin seems contrite and a little uncomfortable. "The accident happened on Highway 99 a little after eight. Another car t-boned yours and sent Ms. Nolan across the median. What's left of your car is in the impound lot."

What's left...

"Sonia's mom's just had hip surgery." My thoughts race, tumbling over one another. Sonia. Hospital. She doesn't have close friends in town. Neither do I. That's partly what drew us together.

Officer Franklin hands me the paper he was holding. My

registration. "Can you tell me what hospital?" I ask, my voice a hoarse whisper.

"Harborview, ma'am. As you weren't driving, you won't bear any liability. But you should call your insurance company."

With a nod, he hurries back to his squad car, and as I shut the door and catch sight of my dinner, still untouched on the counter, I know I won't be eating tonight.

Why do hospitals always smell the same? Doesn't matter if it's the ER, the cancer ward, or the ICU. The scent lingers. Gets under your skin. Inside you.

At the ICU entrance, I press my palms against the counter. "Hi. I'm here to see Sonia Nolan."

"Are you family?" the nurse asks in a bored tone.

"N-no. Just her friend. Inara Ruzgani. She...doesn't have anyone in town except her mother. She was driving my car when she..." My voice cracks and I lean forward. "Can you at least tell me...is she going to be okay? Please."

The nurse softens. "Oh, she's been asking for you. Hang on, love. Let me make sure she's awake." She hands the desk off to another, dour-faced woman and heads through a set of double doors that open and shut with a *whoosh*. As I wait, I stare at my phone screen—at the multiple messages from Royce waiting for me.

Are you okay?

Inara, what's going on?

Call me, baby. I'm worried.

As I debate how to answer, the phone vibrates once more.

I'm coming over.

Fuck. With my fingers shaking, I fumble through a reply.

I'm okay. Friend of mine is in the hospital. Just found out an hour ago. Waiting to see her now. Stay home. Relax. I'll call you when I'm done here.

Shoving my phone back into my pocket, I hold my breath as the smiling nurse pushes through the doors again. "Come with me, dear." She guides me to a desk, where I have my ID scanned and I get a sticker that lets me through the security doors.

Nurse Carol, I learn, has been working at Harborview for twenty years. Maybe that's why she broke the rules for me. As she shows me to Sonia's bed, I have to stifle my gasp.

Her left arm's encased in plaster, her head bandaged, one eye swollen shut. Dozens of cuts mar her pale cheeks, along with the burns from the airbag.

"Inara," Sonia whispers with tears in her eyes. "I lost my phone. I couldn't call you."

She looks so frail in that narrow bed, surrounded by white, her skin mottled with purple and blue, pain etched on her delicate features. "The police found my registration."

"Oh...God. I'm...so sorry."

"Shhh." I lay my fingers over hers, wincing as she whimpers. "I don't care about the car. It's insured. I care about *you*."

"He came out of...nowhere. Never even saw him. Can you... my mom. I can't tell my mom..."

"I'll take care of it, honey. I promise."

Four hours later, after calling Sonia's brother in California, hiring a live-in nurse for her mom for the next two weeks, and reassuring both of them that I'd be there whenever they needed me, I sink down into one of the hard, plastic chairs just inside the hospital front doors while I wait for the Lyft and text Royce.

I hate hospitals. Headed home. Need to crash. Or hit something. Or both. I'm okay. But can I call you in the morning instead?

He doesn't respond right away, and I check the time. *Shit.* It's well after eleven. He's probably asleep. I didn't expect every phone call to turn into four others. Sonia could only stay awake for ten minutes at a time, and between waiting for her to answer questions about her insurance company, her mom's care, and her brother.... Dammit. I should have called Royce earlier.

My phone buzzes to let me know the Lyft driver is here, and I trudge through the hospital doors. Movement out of the corner of my eye draws my gaze, and I freeze with my hand on the car door handle.

The hooded man disappearing around the side of the hospital has a pronounced limp, but the set of his shoulders, his frame, and the messy brown hair peeking out from the black hoodie stir something in my memories.

You're seeing things. Just another hospital visitor heading for the back parking lot. At night. Who was standing still until you exited the building.

"I'll be just a minute," I hiss at the driver before jogging after the man. As I round the corner, I see only a handful of lonely cars bathed in the harsh circles of the bright lights.

I'm exhausted. From the mission and from holding myself together in front of Sonia. Seeing things that aren't there. The Lyft driver honks, and I rush back, apologizing as I sink into the leather seat. "Sorry. It's been a long fucking day."

He only grunts as he peels out, and I'm too tired to care.

When the driver pulls up to my little house, I gape. Leaning against my front door, his hands shoved into the pockets of his winter coat, Royce offers me a sheepish grin as I hurry towards him.

"What are you doing here?" I wrap my arms around his waist, letting the scent of him calm me in ways I didn't know how much I needed until this moment.

"I couldn't wait until t-tomorrow to make sure you were okay." His deep voice rumbles against my cheek, and a part of me wants to rail against being *handled*, but the rest of me doesn't want to be alone tonight.

I stifle my shuddering breath as I dig out my keys. "How long have you been here?"

"Just a couple of minutes."

Pulling back to meet his gaze, relief washes over me as I see the truth in his eyes. I'd hate to think he came over earlier because I didn't answer his texts and just...waited.

Once we're inside, he takes control, asking me where the bedroom is, steering me down the hall, and pointing me towards my closet. "Get into something warm," he says with a gentle kiss to my cheek. "I'll make you—what? Tea? A hot t-toddy? Warm milk?"

"There's a tin of chai in the cabinet next to the stove." The stresses of the past two days have tears threatening, even though I'm about as far from a crier as anyone you'll ever meet. I need to sleep. For a week. If only that were possible.

"Chai it is." Another kiss, this one a slow, lingering press of his lips to mine, and I clutch his arms, unwilling to let him go.

"In a minute."

He rests his chin on top of my head, silently sharing his strength with me, and my heartbeat calms, my breathing steadies, and my fingers finally warm. This...I've never found this understanding with anyone before. Maybe it's the military in both of us. Or...something more. But Royce knows what I need. Whenever I need it.

Pulling away, I force a smile. "I'm okay. Really."

"I know. But that doesssn't mean you can't be better." He takes one step back, then another, his fingers trailing over mine until only the tips touch before he turns and strides from the room, a little uneven, but still one hundred percent in control.

When I emerge, bundled up in my army sweatshirt and a pair of gray fleece pants, I find Royce setting two mugs on my coffee table and holding the blanket I keep on the back of my couch. Wrapping me up, he toes off his shoes and sinks down with me, letting me settle against him.

"Want to talk about it?"

"No."

His flinch is barely noticeable. Hell, if I wasn't pressed up against him like my life depended on our closeness, I wouldn't have sensed a thing. But I know my answer hurt him.

The rich chai warms me, though not as much as being in his arms. "That came out wrong." Tipping my head back, I try to read him, but he's closed himself off. I reach up to cup his cheek, a day's worth of stubble tickling my palm. "Sonia borrowed my car. It was a hit and run. Another driver sent her across Highway 99 and into oncoming traffic. She'll be okay, but...I feel like it's all my fault."

"Was there something wrong with the car?" He slides his fingers up the back of my neck and into my hair.

"No. At least...not that I know of. It was just in the shop after the shit at the warehouse, so it should have been in great shape. But..." I rest my head on his shoulder, suddenly too tired to keep talking.

"It wasn't your fault. Wrong place, wrong time." With his arms around me again and the chai starting to relax me, I drift, not awake, not asleep. Content to just be with this man I'm falling for.

Except...his words hang in the air.

Wrong place. Wrong time.

I've heard them before. Recently. But try as I might, I can't quite remember when. Or why I should even care.

12

——————

Royce

INARA SHIFTS WITH A LITTLE MOAN, her long legs tangling with mine as she's lost in a dream. Halfway through her chai, she fell asleep in my arms, and I carried her to bed.

I don't know what possessed me to show up without calling. Worry. Need. Hers and mine. I spent half the day asleep, followed by hours of fighting with those fucking transmitters. Hell, I ended up destroying two of them when I couldn't maneuver the delicate chips into place.

Old Royce would have thrown the whole lot against the wall. New Royce is supposed to find better ways to deal with his emotions. Or at least, that's what my therapist tells me. All day I'd felt the specter of a seizure looming. I should have stayed home, but Inara needed me. Coming here, being able to take care of my...

I stare down at Inara. Dark circles bruise her eyes. She's lost weight the past two days. Not surprising since she apparently didn't eat tonight. Once I tucked her in, I cleaned up the untouched takeout in her kitchen, finished my chai, and popped a couple anti-seizure pills. But about half an hour ago, a blinding headache woke me, followed by one of the worst attacks I've had in a while. At least it only affected my head. Inara slept right through.

My watch ticks past 3:00 a.m., and I slip out of bed and head for a shower. After an episode, it's the only reliable way to ease the tension.

Stripping, I avoid looking at my reflection as I step under the steaming spray. As the water washes away the memory of waking with my tongue frozen, my neck muscles straining, and my hands clenched into fists, I wonder how much longer we'll go before she has to see me fight through the terror that always comes with an attack. Three years, and it doesn't get any easier.

With my hands braced on the white tiles, I duck my head and close my eyes. Sleeping next to Inara...felt so right. Hiding my seizures? My weakness? My pain?

I tried that once—with Cam. And look where it got me. I want to tell her everything. But...

Small, delicate fingers feather over my hips. Tight nipples press against my back. "I woke up...and you were gone."

Inara molds her body to mine. In a single breath, I'm rock hard, and when she reaches around me to stroke my cock, I groan. "You...should be...asleep."

Fuck.

"I should be underneath you."

She hasn't noticed my awkward speech or the tension in my shoulders. Turning, I claim her lips, my hands sinking into her wavy locks and holding her close.

When we part, both of us breathless, I meet her gaze. "I need you, baby. All of you."

"You have me." When she sinks to her knees, I angle the shower head at my back, trying not to drown her as she wraps her lips around my crown and works her tongue in ways I've only dreamed of.

I fist her hair, but let her set the pace and the tone. The sight of her rocking back and forth, one of her hands clamped on my ass, the other wrapped around the base of my cock, is the most erotic fucking thing I've seen in years, and I try to memorize the look of raw need in her eyes. As she hollows out her cheeks, hums, and cups my balls, my vision goes white, and I can't stop my hips from pistoning violently as I shout her name.

Inara sits back on her heels, looking up at me like I hold the answers to everything when in reality, I'm just as lost as she is. Helping her up, I gather her in my arms and turn her so the hot water sluices over her back.

"Hold me," she whispers.

I press a kiss to the top of her head. "All night."

Once we make it to bed, my headache fading along with the haunted look in her eyes, I run my hand up and down the smooth skin of her back. "I've never been one for having a woman on her knees. But damn."

She chuckles, a low, sexy sound I could lose myself in. "Reason five hundred and three why you're not like other men. That's not usually my go-to move."

"What is?" My dick stirs again, even though I know we should both be sleeping.

"Up against the wall. My legs wrapped around you. Hard and rough."

I squeeze my eyes shut, try to recite baseball stats, count to ten...anything to keep from burying myself deep. She's using sex to distract from what's going on inside—I know because that's exactly what I'd like to do. "You're killing me," I manage. "I just came over to hold you. Be the supportive, understanding partner."

"Partner." Her voice cracks, and she sighs as she lays her cheek against my chest. "I..."

"Building something, remember?" Pressing a kiss to the top of her head, I try to tug the blanket up over the curve of her hip where the last vestiges of her bruise still linger.

Inara tips her head up, longing and raw honesty churning as flecks of blue darken within the gray depths of her eyes. "Royce... what I do...there's always a chance I won't come back."

"I know, baby." I can't help pulling her closer. "But this work... it's a part of you. Who you are. I see that every time you talk about one of your rescues."

"Ryker...he can't stand the idea of letting anyone rot in captivity. Not after what he went through. I just want to *do* something with my skills...something good. And I can save people. Most of the time." Emotion bleeds from her words, like every one of them is a fresh wound.

"Talk to me. Tell me what you wouldn't the other d-day. Why 'most of the time'?"

"Not tonight. Please. Tonight...I just want to feel *alive*. I want to fall asleep in your arms and have one night where the demons don't find me."

Every protective instinct I have flares at the tremor in her voice. I want to shake her, to demand she tell me about those demons that come for her in her sleep. But I don't know that I can refuse her anything, and if all she wants—all she can give me—is this, for the moment, it has to be enough.

I reach over and flip off the light, but as she releases a pent-up breath, I press my lips to her ear. "I'm falling for you, Inara. Hard and fast. This morning...you should know...that happens regularly. I'm dreading the day you see me have a seizure."

Inara wriggles so we're face-to-face, even though her blinds only let enough light in for me to see the outline of her cheek.

"This is all new to me, Royce. Being in a...relationship. But I've seen the worst of humanity. I can't promise I won't fuck something up, but I can promise I won't run."

"I wouldn't blame you. When Cam got blown up, I bolted. As far and as fast as I could."

"Why?" She trails her hand down my arm, then links our fingers.

"Because I couldn't deal with the guilt. I s-s-signed up for the most dangerous assignment I could. On some level, I *wanted* to die. I thought that was the only way I could make things right."

Inara cups my cheek and brushes a kiss to my lips. "I know all about guilt, Royce. You don't have the market cornered."

Playing with a lock of her hair, letting the silky strands slip over my fingers, I wait, hoping she'll continue. She's silent for so long, her slow, rhythmic breathing warm against my chest, I fear she's fallen asleep until she whispers, "When I was twelve, my mother spent ten days in the hospital."

I stroke her back, calming, soothing—or trying to.

"After September 11th, we were living in Newark. One of the planes took off from there. And...things got bad for a while. Our little community—we had a mosque just down the street —was attacked a dozen times over the course of the next few months. In January, my father had to go to London for business, and he begged my mother and me to go with him, but...well..."

"She didn't want to fly?" I try to urge Inara closer, but she shudders and resists.

With a small shake of her head, she continues. "She'd retired years before, but still had friends who worked for Delta and United. They warned her not to. She was so beautiful—still is— but she wears a headscarf, and she is very obviously Middle Eastern. So we stayed home.

"Dad told us not to go outside after dark." She winces like she's reliving physical pain. "I thought he was just overprotective." Pressing her fist against her heart, she says, "I'm an *American*, Royce. I never thought…"

Curling my fingers under her chin, I tip her head up and press my forehead to hers. "Tell me what happened."

"For the first couple of days, everything was fine. But then I forgot to stop and buy bread after school. Mom and I had this huge fight, and she went to the store. On the way home, she was mugged. They hit her over the head, stole her purse, and stabbed her in the stomach. Right outside of our apartment. I…found her."

"Oh fuck, baby. I'm sorry." This time, I don't give her a choice and guide her so she's flush against me, her back to my front, and curl my body around hers. She almost burrows into me, her stuttering breaths not quite dissolving into sobs.

After a few minutes, she calms enough to speak again. "They never caught the guys who attacked her. My father moved us all to San Diego as soon as Mom could handle the trip. New school, gated community…and I started taking self-defense classes. She got hurt because of me. She couldn't have any more children… And she never once blamed me."

"Because it wasn't your fault. But that doesn't make it any better, does it?"

Inara sucks in a sharp breath. "No."

I glance down at her as she blinks, and her eyelashes glisten with tears. "Tomorrow, when you go back to the hospital to check on Sonia, I'm going with you."

Her body goes rigid. "I can—"

"Handle things by yourself? I know you can. But that doesn't mean you have to. You're not alone, Inara. Trust me."

If only I could take my own advice.

13

Inara

THREE DAYS LATER, once Sonia and her mother—along with a private nurse—have both been discharged, I can breathe a little easier. No more hospital visits.

Royce—true to his word—was by my side every time I had to walk through those automatic doors. For someone who spent five years on some of the deadliest combat missions in Afghanistan, you'd think I could handle seeing a friend on the road to recovery, but every day I left with tears in my eyes.

And every time, he held me. Brought me back to his place, cooked me dinner, wrapped me in a blanket on his couch where we watched movies, talked about the little things—music, books, food, and indulged in slow, tender lovemaking that left me soothed, but still needy.

Today, he's tired, though. I can see it in his eyes, the set of his shoulders, the way his left leg drags a little more than usual. I come up behind him in his tiny kitchen and slide my hands over his shoulders. "Sit down. I'll do the dishes later."

With a deep breath, he relaxes against the counter. "Yeah. P-probably a good idea." Dipping his hand into his pocket, he comes away with his pill case, and my heart constricts as he grabs another one of his anti-seizure pills. That's three I've counted today, and I've only spent four hours with him.

The sight of my supportive, confident man popping those pills like candy shakes me out of the fog I've been living in for the past few days.

I urge him into the living room and down onto the couch, where I start kneading those rock-hard shoulders as he groans and stretches his neck until it cracks. "You've been...holding out on me."

"I don't pull out the magic fingers for just anyone." With a laugh—I think my first since I found out about the accident—I bend so I can kiss the sensitive skin behind his ear. "Once I'm done, I'm going home, soldier." He tips his head back as I continue my ministrations, confusion furrowing his brow. "You're exhausted. Rest up, and tomorrow, the real Inara will come out to play."

"Are you sure?" Royce reaches up to cup my cheek.

"Yes. What you've given me these past few days...I can't tell you how much I needed someone in my corner. But you can't keep pushing yourself like this. Working all day, coming to the hospital with me every night, dinners, breakfasts..."

"Everyone needs help sometimes," he says as he tugs my arm so I skirt the couch and drop down next to him. "And you're right. I'm beat. But there's something I need to do before you go."

I lean in, expecting a kiss, but instead, he holds up a small velvet pouch. "Royce?"

"Open it." His voice takes on a rough tone, and words tumble out awkwardly. "I saw this at a booth at Pike Place Market, and when I picked it up, I thought of you. I don't know why—"

"Ohhh." As I angle the bag, a pale pink stone drops into my hand, attached to a delicate silver chain. "It's beautiful." I hand it to him and turn so he can secure the clasp. When the stone touches my chest, it warms almost immediately, and I draw my fingers over the pendant as I face him.

"It's not too soon, is it?" He cups the back of my neck as he brushes a gentle kiss to my lips.

"No. It's not." I straddle him, sinking my hands into his hair as I claim his mouth with a vigor I haven't felt in days. I've never been one for gifts, but with Royce...everything's different.

I have his shirt half off when he suddenly stiffens, and a strangled, pained sound rumbles in his throat.

"Royce?" I pull away, my voice too high, my heart thudding against my chest. He shuts his eyes, fumbling for my hand and squeezing my fingers. The muscles of his neck cord and strain, and tiny lines deepen around his lips.

Oh fuck. I won't panic. I can't. Training takes over. *Assess the situation.* "How bad? Squeeze once for normal, twice for...call an ambulance."

He answers with a single pulse of his fingers, then pulls me closer. I wrap my arms around him, letting him rest his cheek against the top of my head. I can feel his jaw try to work, the muscles flexing, seizing, and flexing again.

"I don't know what to do for you, baby." The term of endearment slips out in a raw moment of terror when he squeezes my fingers again. Pulling back so I can see his face, I hate the look of sorrow in his eyes. "You're still okay?"

He nods, his lips parting slightly, but only a soft "ahh" escapes. Stroking the spasming muscles along his cheek, I hold his gaze.

"Your eyes get these gray streaks in them when you concentrate." I'm rambling, but I love his eyes. I still have the napkin I used to sketch them weeks ago. "When you're about to come, they're almost silver."

His chest stutters with what might be a laugh, and the streaks intensify. Not quite at climax level, but the stress lines around his eyes ease.

"Sssorry," he says, the single word drawn out and thick. "Nnnooo...warning." Sinking back into the cushions, he heaves out a breath. "Over now."

"You're okay?" I've never seen Royce look so...defeated.

With a nod, he closes his eyes for so long, I wonder if he's fallen asleep. I rub his thigh, snuggling closer. I'll sit here with him all night if I have to.

Finally, he shifts and links our fingers. "Cam and I had a system when she t-took care of me after my surgery. One through four. One means I can probably manage a word here and there. This was a two. Three means I need to lie down or I might pass out. If I hold up four fingers, call 911."

"Got it." Still feeling helpless, I rest my head on his shoulder. I need him to know my feelings haven't changed, but that would require me to explain what my feelings *are,* and even I don't have the words for them right now.

"You did exactly the right thing," he whispers. "Thank you."

I run my fingers over the pendant, the smooth stone a warm and solid weight anchoring me. "I'm not running, Royce. I love what we've started, and I'm not going to let anything screw it up."

I pull a fresh canvas from the pile and set up next to the window. I didn't want to leave Royce last night, but he insisted he'd be fine. So I crawled into my bed alone with a cup of chai and a chocolate bar, then stared at the ceiling for half of the night. Despite how well Royce said I'd handled his seizure, I'm not sure I'll feel steady until I see him again. If only I didn't have to wait until tomorrow. But he needs rest, and I need to catch up on work.

I should be neck deep in translations but I'm too scattered, too out of control, and since mind-blowing sex is out of the question, painting will have to do.

The rising sun floods the sky a deep azure the color of Royce's eyes, and I wish I could paint what I see, wish the hope that dawns with the new day could fix this out-of-sorts feeling. Instead, I mix up a dark gray for troubled skies and call upon the storm inside me as my guide.

Next, a muddy brown lays the foundation for a desolate mountain landscape. The rocks emerge, sharp and unyielding, rising starkly against the squall. A solitary tree takes shape, bent in the wind until it's almost folded in two, and before long, I have to be careful where I hold my palette. Tears aren't the best thinner for oil paint.

Yet...despite the pain pressing down on my soul, I'm not alone, and as a single tear drips off my chin and lands on the small, pinkish stone resting below the hollow of my throat, I'm reminded just how lucky I am.

The second I ran my fingers over the pendant last night, I realized I was no longer falling in love. I've fallen. Completely.

Returning to the canvas, I try to outline a leaf blowing away in the wind, but at the end of my brush, another tree emerges. Strong branches reach for the tiny, battle-worn sapling, wrapping it—me—in a warm embrace.

An hour passes. My shoulders cramp, my eyes burn. But when I set down my palette, the image doesn't look anything like what I'd envisioned.

It's us. Or...what I want us to be. Two trees, holding onto one another in the middle of a storm.

"I know you promised to cook me dinner," Royce says when I

crawl into bed and call him late that night. "I heard from Cam about an hour ago. She and West invited us over tomorrow. Along with a couple of folks from Emerald City, one of West's instructors from the dojo, and Ryker. She wouldn't tell me what's going on. If you want to stay in—"

"Oh my God." I clap my hand over my mouth, but it's too late. West didn't expressly forbid me from telling Royce, but if Cam didn't share...

"Inara?"

"We should go. You're going to want to go." A laugh bubbles up, the stress of the past few days along with my shock getting the better of me. "Don't make me tell you what the party's for. Just...*think*, soldier."

"No." The disbelief in his tone stretches the word, and I sink back against the pillows as he huffs. "She used to talk about getting married like it was the scariest idea on the planet. But finding West...best damn thing for her. That's it, isn't it?"

"Yep. West showed me the ring the other day. He was so nervous she'd panic or flat out say no."

Royce chuckles. "She probably still panicked a little."

"I'm surprised he invited Ryker. The man doesn't believe in love. When I told him I couldn't come in for a training op because of our first date, he gave me the whole 'love makes you weak and one day we might not come home' speech."

And now comes the awkward silence. I can see myself with Royce. Long-term. Loving him. Being loved by him. But...something's stopping me from saying the words.

"Inara? Turn on video. I need to see you." Royce's words draw me out of my fog.

Shit. Schooling my features and hoping he doesn't see the self-doubt I can't seem to shake, I hit the FaceTime button. He's shirtless, and the sight of his lean chest and the top of his six-pack drive my fears down deep where I hope they'll stay.

"I could look at you all night," I say with a wistful note to my tone. "You're feeling okay?"

"I just needed rest. What happened yesterday...that's my normal. You can't worry every time I have a seizure or need an early night."

Even over the slightly grainy video stream, I can see the irritation on Royce's chiseled features. "I'm not..." Except, I was worried. I've been worried all day. "Caring for someone...as much as I care for you... It wasn't the seizure. Not exactly. Dammit. I'm not good at this shit." Sliding down under the covers, I balance the phone against my nightstand as I rest my head on my arm. "I should get some sleep. I was up before sunrise."

Sheets rustle as he brings his phone a little closer. His dark brows draw together over those bright blue eyes. "Talk to me, baby. You sound...sad."

"Just dealing with some old demons. I'll be fine in the morning. Rest up, soldier. After the party tomorrow, you're coming back here where I get to have my way with you."

I kiss two fingers and press them against the screen. Royce frowns, but still follows suit with his own goodnight kiss, and as I plug in my phone and turn out the light, I let out a frustrated groan. Intimacy has never been my strong suit, and the question I ask myself ten times a day echoes in my mind.

Why haven't I told him what happened in Colombia?

Tonight, I finally have an answer.

Because I'm scared of losing him. Except...I'm not just scared. I'm terrified.

14

Royce

TEN TRANSMITTERS LINE UP in a row on my workbench. Every one of them perfect. I spent four hours riding the city buses this morning, and each transmitter recorded the exact same data. Well, within a few inches. Civilian GPS data isn't exact.

I tuck one of the transmitters into the back pocket of my jeans. Might as well stress-test the thing. Until I decide how I want to package them—necklaces, bracelets, clip-ons—I figure I should see if they hold up to being thrown in a pocket and sat on for a few hours.

Inara should be here soon, and I toss my laptop and tooth-brush in my briefcase. I'm so close to perfecting the software, I don't go anywhere without the source code. Paranoid? Yes. Despite half a dozen backup copies stored in the cloud, until I submit to the various mobile app stores, Loc8tion's all mine, and I'm not risking her.

This party should be a welcome respite from work, but with how Inara and I left things last night on the phone, I'm worried.

One day soon, she's going to have to tell me about those demons. You don't keep shit like that from someone you...love.

Yeah, I said it. To myself at least. I love her. If I were a betting man, I'd say she feels the same way, but getting her to admit it... I'd have an easier time picking up grains of sand with chopsticks.

She knocks, and when I open the door, I forget to breathe. A shimmering black dress dips low enough to expose the swell of her breasts and the pendant I gave her almost glows against her skin. Slits in the sleeves expose her strong shoulders, and the material clings to every curve, ending above her knees, where black stockings disappear into black, high-heeled boots.

Her lips shine with a deep red gloss and her eyes...my God. The strong, smoky eyeliner turns her gray orbs a bright silver.

"Earth to Royce," Inara says with a small smile. "Are you ready to go?"

"Cam and West won't mind if we're late." I draw her against me, drinking in her scent, but she dangles a set of keys in my periphery.

"Come on. I just picked her up. Want to zip down to the big wine store in SoDo rather than hitting up the neighborhood market?" Her eyes sparkle as she waves her hand towards the curb.

The silver coupe is a few years newer than her previous car, with a black convertible top. "The sales guy was ex-army. I served with his cousin. He gave me a great deal."

I wish I could tell her to slow down. To stop and let me hold her. Under all of the excitement, the makeup, the dress, I see the shadows that shut her down last night lingering. But her smile wins me over, and I sling my bag over my shoulder, lock the door behind me, and follow the woman I've fallen for.

As she parks in front of Cam and West's house, I lean over and brush my lips against her neck. "You've got a little something," I say. "Right here. Is that...paint?"

She angles the rearview mirror and cranes her head. "Oh, shit." Scrubbing the blue smudge with her thumb, she manages to clear most of it.

"Home improvement project?" I capture her hand for one long moment, relishing the warmth of her skin.

With a nervous chuckle, she shakes her head. "Um, after the party, I'll show you. I...um, I paint to relax sometimes."

She doesn't elaborate as she gets out of the car, and I wonder how we've grown so close, so quickly, and she's never mentioned this side of her. But before I can find the words to ask her more, she's ringing the doorbell.

"Hey," West says with a wide smile. I don't know that I've ever seen the guy so happy, and the sounds of laughter follow him down the short hallway. "Come on in."

Orion, Lucas, and Emma from Emerald City are gathered around Cam, glasses of Champagne in their hands, and West heads to the small bar to pour two glasses for us as I say hi to my former employees. It's only a little awkward, the pity in Emma's voice grating along my spine as she asks me how I am. But once I introduce Inara, the focus shifts to her. Another man introduces himself as Anthony Vasquez, one of West's instructors, and I offer him a firm handshake.

"Ryker might not show," West says as he presses a champagne flute into my hand, then holds his arm out to Cam. "And while most of you have probably guessed by now—"

Cam rests her left hand over West's heart and the light catches her ring. "Yesterday, West...uh...asked me to marry him."

"She said yes, by the way," West adds as Cam's cheeks flush and she curls her fingers over his shirt.

Everyone cheers, and we clink glasses, the women crowding around Cam to see the ring, and Vasquez slapping West on the back. I offer West my hand, and when we shake, I pull him in for a quick man-hug. "You're good for her, Sampson. Congratulations."

"I need a minute, in private," he says quietly.

"Everything okay?"

He smiles, emotion welling in his eyes. "Yeah. Help me get the appetizers out of the fridge?" Once we're alone in the kitchen, he shoves his hands into his pockets and cocks his head as he stares at me. "While I was gone...well, it feels like Cam exorcised some of the demons she's been carrying around. She didn't say much, and I won't pry. But you two resolved some shit?"

I fiddle with the transmitter I shoved in my pocket earlier— just to have something to do with my hands. "One of these days, if Cam's okay with it and there's a fair amount of alcohol involved, I'll tell you the whole story. My part of it anyway. But yeah. I can't say we're back to where we were. Probably can't ever get that sort of closeness back once you hurt someone bad enough to lose it. But I told her why I left. The real reason, not the bullshit 'I had another commission' story."

West nods. "That'd do it. Thank you. I know," he says as he waves his hand in dismissal. "You didn't do it for me, and she doesn't need me fighting her battles for her. And she might have said yes anyway. Things changed for us a couple of weeks ago. After Uzbekistan. But the woman wearing that ring is...well, she's whole. Or...at least as whole as any of us are."

I'm not sure I can speak over the lump in my throat. Both because I didn't know how much Cam needed me to step up and because I see that same brokenness in Inara—and until she acknowledges it, I'm afraid she'll always hold a piece of herself back.

After another quick hug, West hands me a tray of fruit and cheese, and we rejoin the festivities in the living room.

"All right. Let me see the rock," I say as I wrap my arm around Cam's shoulders and plant a kiss on the top of her head.

The ring fits her. Understated. Five rubies in a simple silver band. Her lips curve in what I think is an unconscious gesture as she stares down at the sparkling new addition to her wardrobe.

"I'm going to ask you once, Pint." The seriousness of my quiet tone has her pulling away so she can meet my gaze. "You ready for this? A couple of weeks ago...you talked about it like it was the scariest thing in the world."

West was right. No matter what else was going on in her life, good or bad, Cam's gaze always held a hint of restlessness and fear. Now...all I see is her happiness.

"I'm ready for this. I didn't think I would be, but when he asked me—" she huffs out a little laugh, "—the ring was tied to the handle of my mug when he brought me coffee in bed—I knew. He's my home."

When I hug her, she holds on for an extra few seconds. "Please say you'll um...stand up with me when we do this thing?"

"What? As your maid of honor? In a dress?" I pull back in mock horror. "Would I have to shave my legs? Because that's a deal breaker."

She punches me in the arm. "You can wear a suit. Wimp."

"Well, in that case..." I take her left hand, running my thumb over the ring. "I'd be honored."

15

Inara

As I UNLOCK the studio door, Royce's hand on my hip steadies me. I haven't been able to settle since I told him about this side of me. No one knows I paint. Not Sonia. Not West. Not Ryker. I don't share that part of myself with anyone.

"Remember those coping mechanisms I told you about on our second date?" Flicking on the light, I take a deep breath, then lead him over to my little corner.

"I figured you took out your frustrations on a heavy bag or sang off-key in the shower." He presses a kiss to the back of my neck, and I shiver.

"I do *not* sing off-key."

"Prove it." His low, husky voice does something to my insides, and if the studio were a little more private—or had a single soft place to lie down—I'd have his slim black shirt off in a heartbeat.

I hum a few bars of the *Hamilton* soundtrack—badly—and he swats my ass. Turning, I press my hands to his chest, feeling the steady beat of his heart. "I've never shown these to anyone. Sometimes…there's another artist or two in the studio, but they don't really know me."

"Baby, whatever's on those canvases isn't going to change how I feel about you, if that's what you're worried about." Royce cups my cheek, leans in, and kisses me so thoroughly, I can't feel my toes.

But I can't let him distract me, or I'll lose my nerve. When I turn the first canvas around, I bite my lip hard enough to taste blood. Royce takes the painting and sets it on an easel, taking his time studying the swirling waters that seem to swallow up a small island in the middle of a vast ocean.

"When did you paint this?" He traces the brush strokes an inch above the ridges of paint, almost reverently. "It's amazing."

"Two years ago. Bad mission. We lost the target." I can't force my voice above a whisper, and Royce reaches for my hand, linking our fingers. My emotional pain unfolds as I pull out canvas after canvas.

Dark colors, stark angles, bare trees, and rocks…even one painting with a gash through the center that's nothing more than angry splatters of color against a black background. "I fell out of a fucking tree that mission. Snapped my rifle stock in half and broke two ribs. I couldn't manage to draw a straight line—or really…any kind of line. So I just threw the paint on the canvas."

With each piece of my soul I reveal, Royce says less and less, until I pick up the piece I painted after Coop died.

"What happened here?" He wraps his arms around me as we gaze at my pain laid bare. The solitary figure with long, flowing black hair stands at the edge of a cliff, the waters below her red and frothy. Lightning pierces the sky, with a single shaft of sunlight illuminating a path behind her. One covered in twisting vines.

I force myself to clear my throat so he can hear me. "Colombia. When we lost Coop. I…wasn't sure I could ever pick up a gun again."

"Tell me." Royce slides a stool in front of the easel, sinks down, and settles me on his thigh with his arms around me.

My back to his chest, I let his warmth seep into me. "West planned the op. The Colombian president's son was kidnapped by a guerrilla group—the People's Army. Poor kid's only twenty-two. Doesn't participate in politics at all.

"The ransom video..." My voice drops to a whisper. "We see a lot of shit in our line of work. And training teaches us to put it all away. Turn off the emotions. Don't let the target's pain influence our actions. That's always been my superpower." I manage a choked laugh. "My unit called me 'the statue.' I could tune out everything. But after this job...I'm pretty sure I'm more dust than stone."

"Baby, you're anything but dust. What do you think that painting is?" Royce rests his chin on my shoulder as he rubs up and down my arms. "It's you putting yourself back together again."

I tell him everything. Changing the plan at the eleventh hour, Coop's frustration with Ryker at being relegated to backup, seeing West go down, the look of shock on his face as the blood soaked through his fatigues.

"Ryker held him together with duct tape—literally." I chuckle. "I heard them on comms. 'You're a goddamned SEAL, Sampson. If you can't run five hundred yards while bleeding from a stomach wound, you don't deserve to wear the uniform.'"

Royce laughs along with me. "Some of my Special Forces buddies used to say the same sort of thing."

"Coop wasn't where West told him to be. He was across the compound. By the time I saw him...I just hesitated for a second." A tear spills down my cheek. "But that was enough. He went down. I...watched him die."

Royce holds me tighter. "And the painting?"

"I'm stuck. Can't go forward or back. We've had two successful missions since. And I managed to keep myself in check. Be that statue. But every time it gets harder. I'm terrified one day I won't be able to do it. And then...who will I be?"

Turning on Royce's lap, I bury my head against his neck and let go. My tears soak into his shirt, choking sobs scrape over my throat, and I'm shaking. But he just holds me, one hand tracing gentle circles on my back.

When I pull away and start to wipe my nose with the back of my hand, Royce already has a handkerchief in his hand and dabs my cheeks as his deep blue eyes bore into me. "You'll be you. Inara Ruzgani. Translator. Painter. Decorated veteran. The strong, intelligent woman I'm falling in love with."

Neither of us speak as the weight of his words sink in. He almost...

Royce's cheeks flush, and he stammers a little. "You're ssspecial, baby. And I want this relationship to lassst. I—"

Fear grips my heart. I'm not ready to hear him say the words. In part, because I suspect I'll say them right back—and mean them. "Take me home, Royce. Make love to me. Then hold me. All night."

Sex as a distraction? Absolutely. I'm—we're—good at this part. The rest...maybe in the light of day I'll be braver. For tonight, though, my heart's taken enough enemy fire. It's time to retreat.

"Strip." Royce doesn't even give me a chance to drop my phone in the charger before his hands are on me, unzipping my dress, biting along the curve of my neck to send shivers of pleasure straight to my core.

I shrug out of the sleeves, and he cups my breasts, pinching my nipples until I whimper and my thong soaks through.

My knees tremble as he replaces his fingers with his mouth—and teeth. "I fucking love this bra," he says as he switches his attention to the other breast. "But it's got to go."

With one deft movement, he unhooks the front clasp, and the lace falls, the straps catching on my wrists as he pins my hands behind my back. "How thick are your walls?" Another searing kiss leaves me breathless, and I fight to keep my legs from buckling as he backs me up towards the bed.

"Very."

"Take off your stockings. Slowly." Royce bends to help me out of my boots, then steps back so I can release the little clips that hold the thigh-highs in place. Rolling first one, then the other, down and slipping them off, he half-growls when I'm left in only my thong. "That goes too."

Naked before him, I have no defenses when he slides a finger into my slick folds. My eyelids flutter. "You smell like summer," he says, his voice rough. "Open your eyes, Inara. I want you to see everything I do to you."

I obey, and when he withdraws, he brings his finger to his lips and tastes the evidence of my arousal. He grins as he unbuttons his shirt. The muscles under his tattoo shift, and I run my hands over the Army Ranger logo that tops the shattered heart in a pool of tears, then lower to the flames peeking out of his low-slung black jeans.

Sliding my palms along the sculpted planes of his chest, I want to look away from the intensity of his gaze. He sees through me—or perhaps into me—in a way no one has before. After the studio, I should be scared, off balance, out of control, but this man knows me and knows what I need.

His shirt flutters to the bed after I give the soft material a little tug. I'm faster this time and manage to undo all five buttons on his jeans before he can bring my wrists behind my back and hold them there. "Not yet, baby. You're going to come at least twice before you get your hands—or your mouth—on my dick."

I can't go anywhere. Pressed against the mattress, I'm helpless against his greedy kiss. My nipples scrape over his chest, my knees buckle, and he guides me down to the bed, my wrists still pinned in his grasp.

"Okay?" he asks as he presses his body to mine, the hard bulge of his erection sending delicious pleasure arcing through me.

"Uh-huh." I struggle, but I don't want to get away, only get my arms around him, feel the corded muscles of his biceps, dig my nails into his back, show him I need him as much as he appears to need me. "If...you're not...going to fuck me," I say between desperate kisses, "you're going to have to tie me up."

The deep groan that rumbles through his chest makes my heart race, and I jerk my head towards the nightstand. "Bottom drawer."

Royce rolls on his side, keeping me trapped, and yanks on the handle. "You're fucking perfect, Inara. In every way," he says as he pulls out the padded cuffs.

After he kisses each wrist, he buckles the leather around them—loose enough for comfort, but not escape. A hemp rope with a carabiner on each end connects the cuffs to my wrought-iron headboard, and then I'm stretched out before him, naked, wanting, unable to do more than wriggle my hips as he kneels between my thighs.

"What do you like?" He fastens his mouth over one aching nipple, and I arch my back as I cry out. With lips, tongue, and teeth, he tortures the tight bud, and when he slips his fingers back between my legs, I implode, great waves of pleasure drowning out all sound, all sight, everything but Royce, and what he does to me.

His fingers plunge deeper, faster, and then he's nipping my neck, my shoulder. I can't think until he cups my chin, forcing me to meet his dark gaze. "Look...at...me," he growls, then adds another finger. "I want...to see you come."

I can only whimper as he circles my clit with his thumb; I start to keen as he lifts one of my legs and rests my calf on his shoulder, and when he leans forward, pinching the neglected nipple with enough force to make me cry out, I give in to a second, more powerful climax roaring through me.

A light sheen of sweat covers my body, and my over-sensitized skin feels like I'm about to combust. Royce kisses the inside of my thigh, down to my knee, then stretches my leg out on the bed.

I tug at the cuffs, desperate to hold him, to give him half of the pleasure he's given me, but he slides off the bed, and I'm left to watch as he sheds his jeans, then those sexy black briefs. His cock stands at attention, already glistening with his own desire.

"My...turn..." I manage, unable to look away from the most gorgeous man I've ever fucked.

He chuckles as he frees my wrists. "Well, you did come twice."

I stop him before he can climb on top of me, directing him to a short width of uncluttered wall. "Brace yourself."

Royce's gaze turns hungry when I sink to my knees and grab his hips. He twines his fingers in my short locks as I press a teasing kiss to his crown, and once I swirl my tongue along his hard length, he groans and tightens his grip.

"That's it, baby," he says when I take him deeper. "All the way."

Relaxing my throat, I suck him down, running my tongue along the underside of his shaft. When I hum, he lets loose with a string of curses, so I draw back, hollow out my cheeks, and slide one of my hands down to cup his balls. I draw out each stroke until his thighs are trembling and he can't manage more than a few well-placed "fucks" and the occasional "Inara."

Before I can send him over the edge, he twists his hand in my hair. "Stop. God, baby. I'm so close, and I want to be inside you when I come."

As soon as I draw my lips gently over his crown, he hauls me up and claims my mouth. I taste both of us, and the overwhelming need to feel more, do more, say more almost has me confessing the one thing I couldn't say at the studio.

But before I can utter a word, Royce spins me around. "Get on the bed. On your knees. And hold on."

The thrill running down my spine makes my movements jerky, and I'm afraid I'll come if he so much as breathes on my clit, but I do as he asks, watching over my shoulder as he retrieves a condom from the pocket of his jeans and climbs up behind me.

Strong hands palm my ass, warming the skin, and I push back, hoping he'll get the hint. The first slap has me whimpering. By the second, I'm begging.

"Again. Please. Hurt me, Royce. Make me yours."

Four more, and my ass burns in the most delicious way. My channel weeps for him. If I can't have him inside me soon, I won't survive.

As if he can read my mind, he grabs my hips and grinds against me. "I need...you," he says. "T-turn over."

Once I'm on my back, he curses as he fumbles with the foil wrapper.

"Let me." Easing the packet from his hand, I tear it open, and fuck, if rolling a condom onto his throbbing cock isn't the sexiest thing in the world. His eyelids flutter at the contact, his thighs trembling.

"Fuck me," I whisper as I lie back down and scrape my short nails over his hips. "Hard."

He sinks deep in one move, and I gasp as my body struggles to accept his girth. But the delicious pressure starts to build immediately, and I wrap my legs around his waist.

Bracing himself so he can lean down and seal his lips over mine, he starts to thrust. I slide my fingers into his hair, tugging at the short strands as he groans and takes up a punishing rhythm.

As he breaks off the kiss so he can meet my gaze, I find the one thing I never believed I needed, but now don't know that I can live without.

"So...fucking...perfect," he whispers as he reaches between us to find my clit.

"Harder!" I match him stroke for stroke, desperately trying to hold off my release to prolong the all-encompassing pleasure that's turned my entire body into a trembling mess.

"Take me." Royce pinches my throbbing nub. "Take all of me."

Pulling his head down so our foreheads touch and I can see nothing but his deep blue eyes with bright silver streaks, I let go and scream his name.

He falls over the edge with me, my name on his lips, and as he collapses next to me, I think I hear him whisper, "I love you, Inara."

16

Royce

I STRUGGLE AWAKE, the air thick and warm. At my side, Inara
coughs weakly. My sleep-addled brain can't make sense of the
haze in the room until I try to take a deep breath and smoke fills
my lungs. "Fire," I choke out. "Inara! Fire!" Sliding an arm under
her shoulders, I sit her up, and she moans and tries to push
me away.

"Fuck, baby. Wake up. We have to get out of here." A light slap
to her cheek rouses her, and she shakes her head, coughs, and
digs her fingers into my arms.

Her eyes wild, she stares at the smoke hovering in the air for
only a second before she scrambles out of bed. I yank on my
jeans, throw my bag on the bed, and peer out her bedroom door.

"Royce!" Inara tosses me a fire extinguisher, and I try to beat
back some of the flames as she heads for her closet, but in under
two minutes, the damn thing's empty, I can't stop coughing, and
the heat drives me back as the flames lick up the walls to the
ceiling.

I slam the door, then grab the bedspread and wedge it under the door jamb. "Out...the window. N-now."

"I have to get," she struggles with something in her closet, her wheezing getting worse, "my go bag."

"We don't have time." I skirt the bed, not bothering with shoes, but when I try to grab her arm, she shakes me off.

"Go, Royce. Get...out. I'll be right...behind you." She wipes her eyes, and through my own watery gaze, I see her try to enter an electronic combination on a floor safe. She curses as the lock beeps in error.

Striding back to the bed, I rip off a pillow case and tear it into two strips. Once I dump the contents of her water glass over the fabric, I tie one of the makeshift masks over Inara's mouth and nose, then hold the other to my face.

"I can't open the window unt-t-til you're ready to go, baby. The rush of oxygen'll suck the fire right in here."

She swears, then yanks the safe door open. "Got it."

I can only dimly see her heft a large bag over her shoulder, but she rises, so I throw the window wide open and kick out the screen. With a great *whoosh,* the flames attack the bedroom door, and the old, dry wood bursts with orange sparks.

Inara tosses her bag out the window, then grabs my arm and tries to urge me onto the sill. "Go."

"You first."

Her eyes water, but she shakes her head as she glances back towards the bed. "Fuck." She lunges for the nightstand as I try to haul her back. "Please! Just...I need..."

The pain in her voice, even with the smoke clogging her throat, has me releasing her with a prayer. "N-not leaving...with-out...you."

Once she's cradled an old letterbox under her arm, she swivels her legs over the sill, jumps, and lands six feet below, tucking and rolling to her feet with the grace of a dancer. I struggle to get my left leg out the window, my body sluggish, and I all but fall to the ground.

Inara helps me up as a window explodes. We run, as best we can barefoot, barely clothed, and struggling to breathe. Her go bag weighs almost as much as she does. Sirens fill the air as we reach her car, parked on the street thirty feet away. "Royce," she wheezes, "the smoke...de—" More glass shatters and Inara struggles to stop coughing. Flames lick up the west wall. A fire truck screeches to a halt, and in under a minute, water hits the roof.

Wrapping my arms around her, I try to turn Inara so she can't see the devastation, but though she's shivering in just my shirt, she refuses to look away. I'm only in my Levi's, but I don't notice the chill with the heat of the fire.

One of the firefighters approaches, his brow furrowed. "Were you inside?" At my nod, he gestures towards the fire truck. "Come with me. The EMTs are en route. Are you hurt?"

Inara shakes her head and tries to speak, but her words dissolve into a fit of coughing. Though my throat constricts, I manage to force out a single phrase. "Not hurt."

The man, or boy really, leads us over to one of the trucks and urges us to sit on a small ledge while he withdraws blankets and two small oxygen tanks, complete with masks. "Put these on and breathe normally."

Inara stares at her burning home, not acknowledging him, but after I touch her arm, she snaps out of her trance and pulls the mask over her nose and mouth.

Needing to keep her tucked against my good, right side, I fumble with my mask, my left hand clumsy from the stress and the late—or early—hour. After I start to choke again, the mask cradled in my palm, Inara sets the letterbox down and takes care of the elastic strap that holds the mask in place.

The look we share etches into my soul, both of us understanding how close we came to dying. A tear carves a trail through the soot darkening her cheeks.

"Smoke...detectors," she says once we're breathing a little easier. Her usually refined voice bears the strain of the ash and the fear. "Didn't go off."

"When d-did you lassst check them?" Fuck. I run through the mental checklist the doc gave me. No tingling in my neck. No double vision. No headache or pressure behind my eyes. I should be okay. Inara stares up at me with fear darkening her gray eyes.

I answer her unspoken question. "S'okay. Jussst tired. When?"

Before she can reply, the ambulance arrives, and the EMTs hustle us off, wrap us in fresh blankets, check our vitals, and try to get us both to agree to go to the hospital.

Inara stares at the burning shell of her home as the younger tech, a brawny guy named Sal, calls to her. "Ma'am? We need to take you both—"

"No," she rasps. "I can't...leave." She shakes off Sal's hand, pushes off the gurney, and takes two steps onto her small front lawn. I try to follow, but my left leg buckles, and the other guy, Brad, helps ease me back down.

"Sir, with your medical history, we're taking you to Harborview to get checked out."

There's no fucking way I'm leaving Inara tonight. "I'm fine. This amount of a-aphasia is n-normal for t-two a.m." Forcing a deep breath, I push to my feet, sway a little, and ease myself out of the ambulance.

"Smoke inhalation is a serious—"

"No." I glance back at Brad. "I'll sssign whatever I have t-to." The back of my neck tingles, and I dig out my pills, swallowing two dry. "We're...fine. Thank you."

Staggering over to Inara, I touch her shoulder. "Baby, come here." She doesn't move when I wrap her up against me, but I can't let go.

The firefighters work until all that's left of her home is a steaming, darkened shell. While the walls still stand, and they say the back half of the house and garage aren't totally destroyed, the windows, most of the roof, and her bedroom lay in ruins.

"Royce," Inara whispers without taking her eyes off her home. "Everything's...gone."

"Shhh, baby. It'll be okay." Pressing a kiss to her temple, I worry I'm lying. I have to focus on every word, and my vision wavers until I blink hard and blow out a shaky breath.

After the police have our names and numbers and the firemen roll up their hoses and prepare to head out, I take Inara by the shoulders. "Come home with me. I n-need a shower and sssleep. So d-do you. The rest—"

The words are getting harder and slower, and Inara shakes herself out of her haze. "Oh, God. Royce. I'm so sorry." Her voice wavers, and a hitch in her breath tells me she's close to breaking. She wears an expression somewhere between fear and desperation as she digs in her go bag for a spare set of keys.

"N-no," I stammer. "Call a Lyft." She isn't in any shape to drive, and I can barely walk a straight line.

"I can do this. I *need* to do this." Hefting her go bag over her shoulder, she strides towards the car and pops the trunk. With a heaving sob, she braces her hands on the bumper, but before I reach her, she straightens and scrubs her hands over her face.

When she turns, all the emotion has drained from her eyes. "Inara."

"No." Holding up her hands, she backs towards the driver side door. "I'm okay. Let's go."

She's about as far from okay as she can get, but I know that look. I've seen it on Cam's face before. Hell, I've seen it in my own eyes staring back at me in the mirror. Getting behind the wheel will keep her together long enough for me to get us into bed. Everything else will wait until morning. I hope.

Inara

I'm numb. With Royce curled around me, his soft breaths in my ear, I struggle not to tremble. We barely spoke once we drove away from the wreckage of my home—of my life. He tried to draw me out but struggled with every word. When he stumbled climbing the steps to his condo, I panicked, but he swore—slowly and with great effort—that he'd be fine after a few hours of sleep.

The first weak rays of light seep around the blinds. I feel so... safe here...in his arms. Or, I should. But I have too many questions. Why didn't my smoke detectors go off? How did the fire start? My landlord's a jerk, but when the heater went out six months ago, he replaced it with a brand-new unit that required a full electrical inspection.

Shifting slightly, I trace the faint outline of the bruise on my hip.

Wrong place, wrong time.

There's more to this than bad luck.

What if Ryker is onto something? And Sonia? She was driving my car. On a night I was supposed to be in town. Three attempts on my life in a matter of two weeks—in Seattle? I'm not on the battlefield. This is a safe city, relatively speaking, and I live—*lived* —in a safe neighborhood.

The realization that I'm literally homeless causes a sob to well in my throat, and I shove my fist against my mouth to muffle the sound. I'll be okay. I have insurance, savings from my work for Hidden Agenda. But, despite my lack of home decorating skills, I loved my little house in my quiet neighborhood. I can't imagine the landlord is going to rebuild. He'll sell to a developer who'll put up those stupid pod-ments, the mega small apartments that pack ten units onto a lot that used to hold a single-family house.

Royce tightens his arm around me, and I stare down at his hand curled over mine.

"I love you, Inara."

Four words change my entire world. Force me to shift my focus. I didn't show him the last painting. I couldn't. Too raw after my confession, I held back. With my free hand, I trace his fingers. All I can see is him stumbling out of my bedroom window, fumbling for the oxygen mask, leaning on me as we lurched through his door.

Yet, through it all, he was the one who held *me* together. Nudged me into the shower, washed my hair for me as I cried silent tears masked by the spray. We didn't speak as we climbed into his bed, and Royce fell asleep within minutes. Me? My mind won't stop racing.

I shift slowly out from under his arm until I'm facing him. Dark smudges bruise his eyes. A layer of stubble dusts his chin, and a smear of soot lingers on his neck. The sheet pools around his narrow waist. A bullet scar—get shot once and you know exactly what they look like—on his bicep draws my gaze. Shrapnel scars decorate his forearms from the bombs that almost killed Cam.

He grunts in his sleep, his lips twisting into a frown. Under his shuttered lids, his eyes move rapidly, and I lean over and cup his cheek. "Shhh. You're okay, baby." With a sigh, he relaxes. I have no focus where he's concerned. All I see is a man I...love, who almost lost his life because of me.

Tears burn the corners of my eyes—or perhaps that's just more soot. Why did I let him bring me here? What if.... Icy fear spreads through my veins, and I have to get out, get clear, get somewhere I can think. I slip out of bed, then lift my go bag an inch at a time, holding my breath and hoping I won't wake him. This is a conversation I can't have right now.

Once I make it to his living room, I pull out a change of clothes. Black pants, black sports bra, black long-sleeved shirt. My entire wardrobe is in this bag. Three identical sets of clothes —designed for combat and stealth, not everyday. I fold Royce's well-worn Counting Crows shirt with care, intending to leave it behind, but as I look back at his closed bedroom door, then bring the shirt to my nose to inhale his scent, I change my mind and tuck the t-shirt into my bag.

My fingers shake as I lace up my boots. Three attempts on my life. Ryker's godson. I don't believe in coincidences. Not after all I've seen. I find a pad of paper on Royce's kitchen counter and try not to cry as I leave him a note.

The drunk driver. Sonia's accident. The fire. If they're related, every minute I spend here puts you in danger. If someone's after me—fuck. There's no if. I have to figure this out, and I can't do that worrying that you're going to be caught in the crossfire. I'm going dark until I get some answers. I'll check in when I can.

The urge to write "I love you" bubbles up inside, but assuming I survive this, I'd never forgive myself if *this* was how I told him, so I end the note with the incredibly stupid *Yours, Inara xoxo* and then risk tiptoeing back into his bedroom to lay the note on the bed in the space I so recently occupied.

I can't stop my tears from falling as I slip out the townhouse door, and dammit, if I hadn't locked the knob on my way out, I might have gone right back in.

The front desk clerk gives me the side eye as I hand over three worn hundred-dollar bills. "I hate credit cards," I offer in explanation. Tacoma still has a few cheap hotels that aren't flea-infested—or so I hope—and three nights should give me enough time to gain some perspective.

My brief stop at the warehouse for my signal jammer confirmed that no one bugged my car, but I left my new baby at a Park and Ride near Green Lake and took three buses down to Tacoma to be sure.

"Room 227. Up the stairs and to the right," the clerk says as she passes me a keycard. "Enjoy your stay, Ms. Campbell."

Isabel Campbell smiles back at me from the fake driver's license. She's got a passport, too. Credit cards, even a speeding ticket for authenticity. But the less of a trail I leave right now, the better. For once, I give thanks for Ryker's insane demands. Fully stocked go-bags, complete with three different identities, two thousand in cash, clothes, weapons, and ammunition.

Adjusting my sunglasses, I head up the exterior staircase to the second floor, the lump in my throat growing with each step. Once inside the room, I paw through my bag to find one of three fully-charged burner phones. My personal phone probably melted into a big glass lump on the remains of my bedroom floor. With shaking fingers, I use the burner to call my voicemail.

"Inara, please. Come back. You're not alone. I love you."

With ten words, Royce shatters my heart into pieces, and I listen to the message another four times before I cry myself to sleep.

17

Inara

MY ALARM WAKES me two hours later. Pretty sure my eyelids are made of sandpaper. Shower. I need a shower. And a gallon of water. First, though, I have to find out how bad things really are.

Ryker answers my call, and I immediately say, "Toast with jam."

"Fuck." He hangs up, but less than a minute later, the phone in my hand vibrates with a blocked number. I don't speak until Ryker utters the confirmation code, "Pancakes and bacon."

"We're in trouble."

"How bad?" Ryker doesn't *do* small talk, and right now, I appreciate that about him.

"Somewhere between 'we're up shit creek' and 'we're totally fucked.'" As he listens, I recount the full details of the supposed 'drunk driver,' Sonia's accident, and the fire that destroyed my home last night and almost took me and Royce with it.

"Where's your guy?" Clattering keystrokes carry over the line. At least one of us has access to a computer.

"At his place. I...left him a note." Shame keeps my tone low, and I fall back on the bed, staring up at the stained ceiling. I really don't want to know what those discolorations are from. "I couldn't stand the idea of putting him in danger."

Ryker snorts. "Because leaving your burnt-out shell of a house together at two in the morning, exhausted, and driving to his place wouldn't let anyone tail you, right? And whoever this fucker is, there's no way he could have followed you from West's last night? Or seen you with him any of the other times you went out?"

Shit.

He doesn't even take a breath. "I'll head over there as soon as we're done. Give me his address."

I sigh and rattle off the house number and street. "I really hurt him, Ry."

"He's a soldier, isn't he?" Ryker's voice softens just a little, and I don't know that I can take his sympathy. Not now. "He'll understand. Eventually."

I swipe at my traitorous eyes. "Yes—to both. But he's also overprotective as hell and I...love him."

"Well, shit. He knows what we do, right?" After a breath, he makes a frustrated, guttural sound. "Don't answer that. Next time I recruit, I'm making it a requirement. No dating. Are you safe right now?"

Right back into tactical mode. This, I can handle. "Yes. Used one of my aliases, paid cash. I don't have anything but my go-bag. Everything else...burned."

Put it away, Inara. Don't think about anything but the mission. Stay alive.

"I'll get—what's his name?"

"Royce," I whisper.

"Once I've got him locked up tight, we need to meet. As far as I know, West and Cam haven't been targeted, so we're probably looking at someone related to one of our past missions, but I'll suggest Cam stay with Royce until we know what we're dealing with. Come to the warehouse. Be there by 17:00. We'll figure this out. The whole team."

"I don't want to put you, West, and Graham in danger. Outside of Ty..."

"Graham's so new, whoever's after us probably doesn't know he exists yet. West is a SEAL. You think you're going to cut him out of this? Good luck with that." Ryker snorts, and I hear the beeping of an electronic combination lock. "As for me...no one finds me. I find them. Be there, Inara. No heroics. We're a team."

"But..."

"No buts." Ryker pauses, and I think I can hear him rubbing his chin with his palm. "If I know you, you're holed up in some cheap-ass motel somewhere. What happens if you make a mistake? What happens if whoever's after us figures out where you are? You're alone and among civilians. Be there or I'm going to hunt you down myself."

As the line goes dead, I toss the phone back in my bag and sink down to the floor. He's right. I know he's right. So why do I feel like I just signed everyone's death warrants?

Because I don't have perspective.

The more emotions you shove into that box, the harder it is to keep it closed.

My shrink's words haunt me now. Because there's no box in the world big enough to hold my love for Royce. Or the fear that I could lose him.

Royce

"Inara, please don't shut me out. At least text me. Let me know you're not trying to figure this out all alone."

When I read her note this morning, I called West and Cam first thing. But Cam had a big meeting with the CEO of Siren Coffee and West...I wrack my brain. Something to do with his new kids' program at the dojo. If Inara's in trouble, she'd at least call Ryker—wouldn't she?

I slam my hand down on the counter as I realize I don't know. Despite how close we've become over the past few weeks, I can't be sure. The rich scent of coffee fills my kitchen, though I can still smell smoke from the fire. Once I caffeinate, I'll head to West's dojo. He'll know how to get in touch with Ryker.

As the last few drops of a dark Guatemalan blend fill the pot, I fiddle with the transmitter in my hand. Durable little thing. Came through the fire with flying colors—as evidenced by the map I pulled up on my phone a few minutes ago. I need to find a way to make them wearable.

Coffee in hand, I sink down at my counter, staring at the pad of paper and pen. I can still smell her. Even with the overwhelming scent of smoke, a bit of Inara lingers. Lilies and orange blossoms.

I call her one more time, though I don't expect her to answer. "Inara, baby. I just...I love you."

The knock rattles my door half off the hinges, and I jump, my coffee sloshing over the rim of my mug as I end the call.

Before I flip the lock, I ease open the drawer to my little entry table and set my pistol inside. If someone's after Inara, I'm not going to take any chances. Checking the peephole, I frown. I don't recognize the man outside. Short brown hair under a black baseball cap, loose cargo pants, and a black sweater that doesn't do much to hide his bulk. With my hand on the gun, I take a step back.

"Royce, my name's Graham. I work with Inara. Ryker called me. Told me to come get you."

Graham. I try to replay the conversations we've had about her work. "Where was your last mission?"

"Mexico."

That checks out. And from what Inara told me about Ryker and their operation, there's no way anyone outside of their team would know where they went. "Have you heard from Inara?" I ask as I throw the door open.

Graham glances back at the street before pulling his baseball cap down a little farther. "Can I come in?"

Sliding the drawer closed, I step back and wave him inside. "She won't return my calls. The fire—" A dry cough chokes me, and I brace my hand on the wall. "Sorry. Is she okay?"

"She's safe," he says as the door clicks shut. "Ryker sent me to get you. Until the team figures out who's after them, everyone's holed up at a safe house. Pack a bag, and I'll bring you to her."

I turn, and three steps into the hallway, a brick wall slams into me. I go down, hard. The punch to my kidney steals my breath, and I wheeze as I try to turn over, kicking Graham and catching him in the shin. He swears but lands another strike to my solar plexus. "You're coming...with me."

"Fuck you." I manage to catch him in the jaw with a weak uppercut, but that only pisses him off. He's got at least thirty pounds on me—if not more. Another punch and I see stars. I'm not going to win this fight. With one last burst of strength, I roll him off of me, push myself up, and stumble towards the door, desperate to reach my gun. Graham locks his arm around my throat and we crash into the kitchen counter, knocking my coffee mug over and sending the still-steaming liquid splashing onto the floor as he hauls me back against him.

"I don't think so," he growls as he tightens his grip. "You're my leverage."

I give up clawing at his arm and lunge for my phone, but he

spins me as my fingers brush the screen. The phone clatters to the floor, and Graham slams his foot down on top of it with a sickening crunch. My vision darkens. I've lost. And God help me, I don't know if I'll see another day. "Inara..."

"Yes. Inara," comes the rough voice in my ear. The world starts to slow, and my thundering heartbeat half-obscures his next words. "You're going to help me get to her."

No. God, no.

He's going to kill her.

As consciousness slips away, I have only one thought.

I wasn't strong enough.

18

Inara

THE PHONE RINGS, startling me awake. The clock on the nightstand is blurry, and I rub my eyes. I still have two hours before I'm supposed to meet Ryker at the warehouse. Why's he calling me now? No unauthorized contact. His rules.

"What?" I don't bother with the code words. He's the only one with this number.

"We've got a problem. How fast can you get here?" Ryker shushes someone in the background.

"I don't have a car. An hour by bus." My hands start to shake. "Ry…"

"Tell. Her," West snaps. "Or I will."

"Royce is missing."

How did I end up on the floor? My ass hurts. The room spins around me, and I can't work my throat to make a sound as my heart threatens to shatter into pieces.

Ryker shouts through the phone still clutched in my hand. "Inara! Focus. Where the fuck are you? Which hotel? West and I are coming to get you."

I blink hard, even though raising the phone feels like picking up a fifty-pound weight. But I manage to glance over at the land-line on the bedside table. "Narrows Inn and Suites. What...happened?"

Tires squeal, a horn honks, and Ryker lets loose with a string of curses. "Fucking hell, West. You're going to get us killed before we even get out of the city."

"Put her on speaker."

I've never heard West so angry—or scared, I can't tell. "What happened? West, please."

"Listen to me, Inara. We're headed to you in a black Thunder-bird. ETA thirty minutes in this fucking traffic. Gear up. We don't know who's after you—or whether it's you or all of us. Graham's in Canada for the week, and he's safe. But when Ryker got to Royce's condo, no one was home, and there were signs of a strug-gle. He's not answering his cell—it's going straight to voicemail."

"Oh God. West...if I lose him..."

"Stop that," Ryker snaps. "You have twenty-nine minutes. Take a cold shower. Get your head on straight. That's an order. If you can't pull it together, we could all pay the price—including your man. Do you understand?"

"Yes, sir." Orders, I can follow. Disconnecting the call, I strip on my way to the shower.

I finish wiping down the room and peer out a slit in the drapes. Two minutes later, a black car pulls into the parking lot, and I'm out the door with my go bag banging against my still-bruised hip.

"Tell me everything," I say as I climb in the backseat.

"Fucking fire. I've been asleep half the day." There's no room for emotion now. If Royce is still alive, I'm not going to find him by falling apart.

West spares a single glance in the rear-view mirror as he swings the car around. "Cam's with Lucas at a hotel in Shoreline under one of my aliases."

"Lucas? The big guy with the dreads?" I met him at their party. He's almost as tall as Ryker, easily as built as West, and a total sweetheart.

"No one messes with him. Even though he can't throw a punch to save his life."

"And Royce?" My voice cracks, but I shove the momentary panic back down where it can't compromise the mission—and Royce's life.

"No word. Cam's trying to hack into the traffic cameras around his condo, but it's taking her some time. If there's a way to find out where he went—or if someone took him—she'll do it."

Digging my nails into my palms, I use the pain to keep me centered. "What did you see, Ry?"

He lowers his voice, sitting like a statue in the front seat so I have to strain to hear him. "Door wasn't locked. Closed, not locked. Broken stool by the bar. Coffee spilled all over the counter. A few drops of blood on the wall. Like from a couple of punches. And his phone and watch in pieces on the floor."

With a small shake of his head, Ryker glances over at West. "Found a Glock in a cabinet by the front door. He was prepared for trouble. Don't know why he didn't use the damn thing."

"What the hell, man?" West punches the gas, merging onto the freeway as the setting sun paints the dark clouds gathering in the western sky in burnt orange and a sickly green. "You didn't mention that."

"We've been a little busy."

"Enough. Both of you," I snap. "Royce is—" I swallow hard, "—careful. He keeps his gun in a safe in his closet. He probably took it out after my note. But if he didn't use it, whoever took him was able to convince him to open the door without protection. Who could do that? Royce and I don't have any friends in common besides Cam and West."

"Someone who was able to convince him you were in trouble," Ryker says.

West shoots me a quick glance in the mirror. "Royce left me two voicemails this morning when I was teaching. He was out of his mind worrying."

Fuck. "I screwed up. Don't you think I know that by now?" Fiddling with the handle of my go bag, I stare down at my shaking fingers. "I shouldn't have left him. I wasn't thinking. I..."

West says my name sharply, and I clamp my mouth shut. "This isn't helping. As soon as we get to the warehouse, we need to focus on finding this asshole. We still don't know who he is or what he wants, other than you. And maybe Ryker. No one's come after me."

"Yet," Ryker mutters.

I've been so wrapped up in my fears for Royce that I never even asked about Ryker's godson. "Is Ty okay?"

He flinches, then turns to stare out the window. "He's safe."

That's a no, then. The kid sobbed in Ryker's arms half the way to the airfield. He's going to need some serious counseling to get through the shit the cartel did to him.

"All right," West says as he takes the offramp for Corson Ave. "Time to put it all away. Both of you. Whoever this asshole is, it's possible he's watching the warehouse. We're going in hot, grabbing guns, laptops, and gear, and getting the hell out of there. Seven minutes tops. One of us watches the car at all times. Ryker, you and Inara go in first."

The car squeals to a stop five feet from the door, and Ryker has his gun drawn before his feet hit the pavement. "Go now," he growls at me, and with my hand on the butt of my own pistol, I head for the keypad, trying desperately not to hear Royce's voicemail over and over in my head.

Inara. Please come back. You're not alone.

Royce

Awareness returns slowly. Along with pain. A roiling vortex in my gut that threatens to send what little I have in my stomach for a ride. My shoulders burn, and breathing takes all the effort I have.

I try to remember how I got here, but there's nothing after an arm around my throat, the crunch of my broken cell phone, and my last-ditch effort to save myself—and Inara.

Panic wins out over pain and exhaustion, and I force thoughts of Inara away. Down deep where my captor can't take them, can't use them against me.

Assess. Plan. Act.

Falling back on my training, I take stock of my body. I'm on my knees, on hard metal. Ankles bound. Still wearing my shoes. I can barely wiggle my toes. The lower half of my body is already going numb. Every breath sends daggers of pain shooting along my ribs, my shoulders, my chest.

A spasm races through me, and something hard bites into my wrists. Zip tie. My foggy brain can't make sense of it all. How am I upright? Struggling for another breath, I find my answer as I turn my head.

Fuck.

A rope creaks as I sway slightly, and the room spins as I realize what he's done. The pain in my shoulders. The heavy weight on my chest. My arms are pulled high, almost parallel to the floor. Stress position. Designed to inflict maximum pain with minimum effort. I can still feel my fingers, so I haven't been tied up like this very long. A few hours like this, without respite, and I might never have full use of my arms again.

Whoever this asshole is, he's been trained in advanced interrogation techniques. My breathing is already a little strained. It'll get worse the longer I can't move. Straightening my back as best I can, I grit my teeth against the dizziness that threatens.

Get your bearings. Find a way out.

Who am I kidding? Even at full health, escaping a stress position is damn near impossible. Still, I blink hard, trying to clear my vision. A bright light shines in my face, but to my left and right, I catch glimpses of dark metal walls. Not far away. Ten feet across, maybe.

I jerk in my bonds as a heavy lock *thunks* behind the bright light. Metal screeches, a door perhaps, and I try to squint but lose my balance and fight not to fall over. My groan echoes from the walls.

"Awake, finally?" The door slams, and as my attacker reaches me, he snaps his fist against my side. "Good. We've got work to do."

"Fuck...you," I gasp as I fight to spread my knees a little to center myself.

He chuckles as he grabs a metal chair, spins it around, and sits with his arms draped over the back, fingers laced together. Burn scars peek out from his shirt sleeves and a bright, red line curves from his temple to his jaw, close to his ear. I don't know how I missed it before.

"Who...are you?" I say, my words thick as the stress and the pain converge in a headache that has me struggling not to pass out. The back of my neck tingles. Fuck. I'm headed for a seizure, and I doubt asshole here brought my pills.

"My name isn't important," he says as he rubs the scar near his eye. "I don't have one anymore. Not after what they did to me. I'm a dead man." He angles the chair, then extends one arm. The snap of a pocketknife sends a tremor along my spine, but asshole doesn't get up. With sick fascination, he pushes the knife against his skin.

Blood wells, then starts to drip onto the metal floor. The knife slides in deeper, between the two bones of his forearm, and when the tip breaks the skin on the other side, he smiles. "They tortured me for so long, something broke in my head. I don't feel pain."

He yanks the knife free, and the bright light glints off the blood. "Do you know what that does to a person, Royce?" Pushing the blade closed against his thigh, he shakes his head, then pulls out a lighter. Cauterizing the wounds, he wrinkles his nose at the horrible stench of burning skin that fills the container. "Makes you wonder if you're still alive."

"What d-does this have t-to d-do with Inara?" I stammer.

He meets my gaze, his eyes bloodshot, wild, and almost...gleeful.

"Everything."

19

Inara

ROYCE's last voicemail message to me was five hours ago. I play it again, over and over, as West navigates the Thunderbird through the rush hour traffic. He has a buddy who works in real estate, and he called in a favor. We're headed for a vacant, private building in Georgetown, where his friend said we could hole up for at least twenty-four hours.

If we don't find Royce by then...

"I love you." I fumble for the "replay" button, but my hands aren't steady, and I miss, letting two seconds of dead air play before he disconnects. Except—I hear something.

"Ry. Listen to this." I put the audio on speaker, then play the message again.

"Why are you torturing yourself like this?" West asks.

"Shut up. Listen."

With the volume at maximum, Royce's final words to me fill the car. But a second after his "I love you," there's a knock in the background.

"Son of a bitch came at him through the front door." Ryker shakes his head. "Ballsy. I'll give him that."

West's phone rings, and he puts the call through the hands-free. "On speaker, angel."

"Got something," Cam says, her voice strained. "How long until you're at a computer?"

"Five minutes." Angling the car into an alleyway, West pulls up behind a dumpster. "Call you back from inside."

"You better. In ten, I'm calling the cops."

Ryker raises a brow at West. "If she—"

"If it takes us longer than five minutes to get back to her, we're probably dead or in serious shit," I say to try to diffuse the situation. "Come on. Every minute we spend bickering is a minute Royce might not have."

Hand on the butt of my gun, I climb out of the backseat and head for the cheap lockbox on the back door. West relays the code, and we're in. Less than three minutes later, West has a laptop set up and launches a video call with Cam.

"We're here, angel. Send me what you've got."

She and Lucas hover around her laptop, cheap hotel curtains in the background. "There aren't any traffic cameras within a six-block radius of Royce's condo. But his neighbor has one of those stick-up security cameras. And she's a talker. Woman wouldn't shut up when we were there taking care of him after his surgery. I know the street she grew up on for fuck's sake, along with her dog's name, her favorite teacher...mother's maiden name... Anyway..." Cam shares her screen, and a man dressed all in black passes by the camera, his head down, at 11:42 a.m.

"That's it? That could be anyone," I say, squinting as the video loops.

"Yeah. It could be. But what goes in? Eventually has to come out."

A second video loads, and the man wheels a large suitcase down the street. Large enough to stuff a body in. The suitcase catches on the uneven sidewalk and nearly topples over. In his haste to right the bag, he must forget about the camera, and Cam stops the video on a semi-clear shot of half his face.

An angry red scar traces the side of his cheek, and brown hair peeks out from underneath the baseball cap. I freeze, and all the air leaves the room in a *whoosh* as Ryker and West swear in unison. "Is that...?" West asks.

I don't have to wonder. That face haunted my nightmares every fucking night for more than three months. Every time I closed my eyes—until Royce came into my life, and then...they eased.

But I'll never forget. Because I watched him die.

I find my voice, but it's so weak, I doubt the other two even hear me as I whisper, "Coop."

"How the *fuck* is he alive?" Ryker grabs my shoulders and shakes me out of my trance. "You said you saw his body."

Tears burn my eyes, and I blink hard to clear them. "I watched him *die*. I had one of them in my goddamn sights, but you were shouting in my ear about West bleeding out, and I hesitated. Just for a second. I hesitated, and the asshole shot Coop in the chest." The lump in my throat makes it hard to speak, but I force the words out anyway. "I watched the life leave his eyes. Drew down on his chest just to find out if he was still breathing. Five seconds. And nothing. Then you and West were taking fire again, and I hauled ass out of there to try and save at least some part of our fucking team."

"Well, he looks pretty goddamned good for a ghost." Ryker slams his hand on the table, rattling the laptop.

"Hey. We're still here, remember?" Cam's voice sounds tinny

through the speakers, but her annoyance is loud and clear. "And Royce is still missing. Sort this shit out later, soldiers."

"That's my girl," West says under his breath as he scoots his chair closer. "So where did they go?"

"No fucking clue." The picture of Coop disappears, and Cam's worried face fills the screen again. "But if this *is* your teammate, and he's blaming you for whatever the hell happened to him after you left, all three of you need to check your phones. Now. He's got a plan and Royce is part of it. Ten bucks and a top-shelf bottle of bourbon he calls and demands something in the next couple of hours if he hasn't already."

"Thanks, angel. Keep this phone on, and don't leave the hotel room, okay?" West's voice softens, and he brushes his fingers close to the computer's camera. Cam mirrors his motion a second before the feed cuts out.

With a few keystrokes, West brings up a program that looks a lot like a cell phone. "Cam hooked me up with this," he says. "It'll let us spoof our cell phones without giving a traceable GPS signal. Inara...he'll probably call you before me or Ryker."

"What do I do?"

After he keys in a long string of digits—the code from my SIM card, apparently—West pushes away from the table, stands, and holds the back of the chair for me. "Click the home button, then enter your lock code. The emulator will do the rest."

It takes me three tries to get the mouse over the stupidly small on-screen button, my fingers are shaking so much. West lays his hand on my shoulder, giving me a reassuring squeeze. "You're not alone."

"Inara, please. Come back. You're not alone. I love you."

Swallowing my emotions, I type in my passcode. Half a dozen notifications scroll by. Including a text message from an unknown number. Glancing up at Ryker, I draw strength from the hard set of his jaw and ice in his blue eyes. I can do this.

"Oh God."

A blazing light shines down on the crumpled body of the man I love. His wrists and ankles are bound, his eyes closed. The message under the photo makes my blood run cold.

Your luck just ran out.

They say your life flashes before your eyes when you're about to die. But the two times I've seen the events of my past speed through my memories, it's been someone else's life on the line.

My mother. As she lay bleeding on the pavement outside our apartment, I saw my childhood. Sitting on her knee. Making chocolate chip cookies and flinging tiny pinches of flour at each other. Seeing her standing proudly and clapping at my grade school talent show after I gave a very bad performance of "Tomorrow" from the movie *Annie*.

And now Royce.

My eyes burn as I see his face. Hear his voice. I touch the pendant I haven't taken off since he fastened it around my neck. His fingers dance along my spine. His lips feather over the shell of my ear.

"Inara."

West's voice cuts through the fog. "Inara. Engage him. We need to know if Royce is alive."

With a shudder, I refocus on the screen.

Show me proof of life.

On screen, *blocked number* flashes as a shrill ring makes us all jump. When Coop's face coalesces on screen, I grip the edge of the table.

"The gang's all there, I see." His voice is rougher than I remember. Bags gather under his eyes, illuminated by a harsh light. The scar alongside his face is bright red, still puckered, as if it's only recently healed. If I had to guess, he's lost at least thirty pounds, but he's still a hulk.

"Where is Royce?" I try to keep my voice from cracking, but I'm only marginally successful. "If you've hurt him—"

"Oh, I've definitely hurt him." Coop takes a step back, and my heart skips a beat. West's fingers tighten on my shoulder, warning me not to lose my shit.

Blindfolded, duct tape over his mouth, Royce wavers on his knees, his arms pulled high enough behind his back that he's struggling to breathe. His head bobs, and he shouts something unintelligible from behind the tape.

"Cut him down. Now."

"Can't do that." Coop slaps his hands down on Royce's shoulders and pushes him forward. The scream that rips from Royce's throat tears me apart.

"What do you want?" I cry.

With a crooked grin that makes his eyes glint in the spotlight, he gestures to the screen. "You. Be at the coordinates I'm sending you in twenty-three minutes, or I start turning this winch. How long do you think it'll take for lover boy to suffocate? I hear it's one of the most painful ways to die. And come alone. If I see even a hint of Sampson or Ryker, I'll put a bullet in his brain."

The gun presses to Royce's temple, and I can't get the words out fast enough. "I'll be there."

As the call disconnects and a set of GPS coordinates flashes on the screen, West grabs the laptop and plugs the numbers into Google. "The fucker knows where we are."

"What?" Ryker and I say in unison.

The look he gives me could freeze lava. "We're twenty-one minutes away. Get in the fucking car. Now."

West takes a corner on two wheels, slamming me against the passenger door. In the backseat, Ryker rummages through our go bags, pulling out magazines, holsters, and earbuds.

"He's been planning this. He knows us. How we operate," West says as he lays on the horn. "And I don't know a damn thing about him. I can't predict—"

"It's six-twenty. He's had Royce for a little over six hours. Found out I didn't die in the fire eight hours before that. He's had plenty of time to set traps all around the rail yard. And he ran comms. He'll have a signal jammer," I say as I accept the shoulder holster from Royce and stare at the straps in my hands. "He's not going to let me keep any weapons."

"Probably not, but you're sure as fuck not going in there unarmed," Ryker growls. "Take off your shirt."

"What?"

"Lean forward and take off your goddamned shirt."

I do as he asks, and Ryker presses a flat blade against my spine, then spreads duct tape over the knife. "Here. Tape this one between your breasts."

"Lovely." I suppose it's good I'm not overly curvy. I'm not sure how this is supposed to help me. Reaching the knife at my back might work. The one between my breasts? Still, I press the tape against my skin, then tug my shirt back on before accepting an earbud from Ryker's outstretched hand.

"Test, test, test," he says.

"Roger."

West slows as we approach the rail yard from the south and ducks into an alley between two tall buildings. "Five minutes to go. Ryker and I'll take positions up high." He shows me his phone screen. "I can track you. At least until he jams us. Once I get the lay of the land, I'll—"

I reach out and grasp a shoulder of the two men. "Promise me," I say, my voice cracking and tears gathering in the corners of my eyes. "You'll get him out safely. Don't worry about me. Royce is the priority. Do you understand?"

Ryker starts to object, but West shoots him a look, and he nods. "We'll find a way. Whatever we have to do."

"Don't get dead," West says. He claps his hand over mine, squeezes once, and then he and Ryker are gone, and I'm alone.

"I'm coming, Royce," I whisper as I slide over to the driver's seat and throw the car into drive.

Cam managed to clone my cell phone on the first five minutes of the drive, and as I step through the gates of the train yard, I tuck the Bluetooth into my free ear.

The phone rings a minute later. "Right on time."

"I'm here. Now let Royce go." There's no video, and in the fresh darkness of early evening, I can't see anything but railcar after railcar after railcar. Each well over fifty feet long and ten feet wide.

"Head east. Did you really think it would be that easy?"

"No." I start forward slowly, my hands at my sides. "But can you blame me for asking?"

"Keep him talking. Keep him distracted." West's low voice in my other ear calms me.

"What happened, Coop?"

"You left me for dead. Do you have any idea what the People's Army does to prisoners? They had me for seventy-three days. And I spent every one of them planning how I was going to kill you."

Emotion. I can use that. "I watched you die," I cry. Let him think I'm as unstable as he is. Right now, the whole train yard could burst into flames around me, and I wouldn't react. Strange.

I've spent so much of the past three months worried I couldn't turn off my feelings, and now, I'm detached, cold, ready to act. "Saw the blood. You weren't breathing. I never would have left you if—"

"Bullshit. We worked together for what? Six months? And very first mission with the new guy, you're laughing and joking around with him, and I'm off tactical. You never liked me. Neither did the Neanderthal."

"He's fucking dead," Ryker mutters.

"You were the one who went off book. Why weren't you backing up West and Ryker?" I fight my cringe as I bait him, but I've got to keep him distracted.

"Take a left between those two train cars," he says sharply. I force a deep breath as I turn a three-sixty to scan for any sign of him—or the rest of my team. I should know better. I wouldn't see West and Ryker if they were right on top of me. We're better than that. Then again, so was Coop—when he followed orders. "When you get to the end of the row, take four steps forward and stop."

"I don't have a visual." The tension in West's voice grates along my spine. "Stop before you leave the row. Let me get into position."

If I don't do exactly as Coop says, he'll know I'm not alone. That I'm on comms. I can't risk Royce's life.

"I'm not stepping out into the open unless you prove to me that Royce is still alive." Forcing strength into my words, I press my back to one of the train cars. The cold seeps into my skin through my combat gear. The feel of the knife between my shoulder blades reassures me that I might get close to him without being totally disarmed.

The phone in my hand buzzes, and I accept the video call. Royce stares into the camera, desperation in his tired blue eyes, as Coop fists his hair. His gaze darts down to the floor, up and down, at least four times—warning me of something, but too soon, Coop lets go, and Royce moans weakly as his chin sinks towards his chest.

"Good enough? Now put the phone in your back pocket and step out into the open." His sneer makes me want to knock his teeth out, though I think someone's already done half the job for me.

As I slide the phone into my pocket, my comms click. "We're too far away for a shot. Stall him."

"Move, Inara. Or your boyfriend here pays the price."

I step out from between the train cars, and a set of bright lights comes on, blinding me. Still, I advance four paces, then freeze with my hands at my sides.

"Weapons. All of them. And the earbud." Coop knows what I usually carry. The pistol strapped to my thigh. The knife lying against my calf. The backup piece in a holster on my left ankle. He orders me to lift up my shirt, and I hope to all that's holy that he'll stop at the bottom of my bra. At that point, I might be able to keep the blades. "Now turn around in a circle. Slowly."

"I'm not your goddamned trained monkey. Let Royce go. I'm here. Unarmed." Still, I spin slowly until I'm facing the harsh lights again.

"Start walking. I'll tell you when to stop."

Unable to see where I'm going, cut off from my team, I take slow, careful steps. Until fifty feet away, the edges of another train car start to coalesce. A fainter light shines from inside, and I speed up as I think I can make out Royce's silhouette.

When I'm sure it's him—fuck, he's half hanging by his arms now—I start to run, just as three *pops* sound from the west side of the rail yard. I can't stop. There's no cover between me and the car Royce is in, and I have to get him out of there.

"I thought you'd like to know, Inara," Coop rasps over the call. "Ryker's down."

"You motherfucking piece of shit," I yell as I leap into the train car. Royce shakes his head wildly, and I know why—a second too late. My foot catches on a tripwire I couldn't see with the lights blinding me, and I go down, hard. On a metal plate that clicks. "Fuck. Fuck, fuck, fuck," I scream as the rail car doors slam shut, sealing me and Royce inside.

"That's right, sweetheart. You just activated the bomb. Open the doors, it'll go off. Move, it'll go off. Oh, and in case you're counting on Sampson rescuing you—" Four more shots, rapid fire, "—I've got him pinned. And you have four minutes...well, more like three minutes and fifty seconds left to live."

The call disconnects, and I look at the man I love, tears welling in my eyes. "Royce. I'm sorry. I'm so sorry."

20

Royce

WHEN THE ASSHOLE—COOP, I now know—let Inara see me without the blindfold, I prayed she'd somehow understand the only warning I could give her, but as she lies sprawled on the pressure plate, tears in her eyes, I strain at the rope holding me. If I could get free...I might be able to disarm this fucking bomb.

My shoulders send sharp, electric bolts of pain down my arms, and I scream behind the tape. I can't even tell her I love her.

Inara groans as she gropes at her back, and I stop struggling, confused. A faint ripping sound and then she's holding a blade as wide as my palm. She swipes at her eyes, brushing away the tears balancing on her lower lids, then narrows her gaze at the winch and rope torturing me with every breath.

Before I saw her face on camera, I'd almost given up. I couldn't keep my back straight any longer and tried to alternate the pressure on my arms with that on my spine. But every time I forced myself upright, it got harder. Each breath was torture, and I'd started to wheeze. Moments before she started running towards the train car, I had my second seizure, and I don't know how much longer I can stave off another one. Though, in three and a half minutes, it won't matter.

"Please," she whispers, takes a deep breath, and throws the knife. It nicks the rope but leaves one strand of the weave holding on. "No!"

Fuck this. With a roar that would sound a lot more impressive without the duct tape over my mouth, I jerk my arms and fall to the side, ignoring the agony in my left shoulder. Shock steals my breath as I hit the ground, the rope snapping and coiling against my arm as it falls.

Except...my lower body is numb. My arms are practically useless, still tied behind me. I twist, looking for the knife, but Inara screams my name. "I have another one. Just get the fuck over here. Please!"

Her hand dips down the front of her shirt this time, and I roll myself closer until I feel the edge of the pressure plate at my hip. The zip tie snaps in half, and I whimper as my arms fall free. She cuts the tie around my ankles next, then rips the tape from my lips.

"I'm so sorry," she sobs as she leans down and kisses me. Short, desperate kisses over my lips and cheeks pepper her words. "I should have told you...before the fire, after we made love, or at my studio, or when you gave me the necklace—"

"Nnnot...nnnow," I slur. I'm so messed up there's no way I can reply the way I want to. "Bomb."

My left arm hangs uselessly at my side, the shoulder dislocated and likely permanently damaged, and my right hand is half-numb. But I fumble for the blade in her hand, just as another seizure barrels into me, splitting my head in two with the pain and stealing the vision in my left eye.

I half crawl, half roll to the center of the train car. Unable to make a sound, I wrench the floor panel up and meet her gaze with a weak nod.

"Holy shit." Pulling the phone out of her back pocket, scowling at the broken screen, and then tossing it aside, her eyes widen. "Two minutes. Tops."

I can do this. It's a simple dual circuit detonator. I watched the fuckstick put it together. First, the timing mechanism. One screw, then another, then another, and I send a metal plate flying to expose a dozen wires. My depth perception is shot until the seizure releases its hold on me, and I squint, curse silently inside my fucked-up head, and look back at Inara.

Please understand me, baby. I love you. With everything I am. But I need you right now. Help me through this.

"Talk to me, Royce."

I hold three fingers to my temple, my jaw muscles straining as I fight my way through my body's betrayal. The other night… she'd done more than she could know just by distracting me from the sheer terror of being unable to speak.

Focus. One wire at a time.

Inara starts talking as I turn back to the bomb. "When this is over, we're going to go up to Salish Lodge. We'll get one of those ridiculously expensive rooms with the soaking tubs for the weekend. A couple's massage. Breakfast in bed. Hell, room service for every meal. No clothes other than bathrobes. Spend as much time as we can naked."

Four words into what she wants to do to me, her voice cracks and she clears her throat. I slice through the first wire, my heart stuttering until I count to three and realize we're both still alive. She describes a spring trip to Vancouver for dim sum and sushi, and my fingers shake as I slide the blade under the next wire. "And then it's baseball season. I didn't even ask if you were a Mariners fan. My boss has box seats, and he lets me use them every couple of weeks."

The lump in my throat swells as another spasm rolls through me, and I almost catch the tip of the knife on the wrong wire—

one of the four that would set off the bomb in an instant. But I recover, and the last wire snaps in two.

Tears roll down my cheeks, silent sobs wracking my battered body. The tight band around my skull loosens with a hiss, and my tongue no longer feels like a lead weight in my mouth. "D-don't move," I slur, my words so slow and unwieldy, I don't know if she can understand me. "Got t-timer. N-n-not plate."

Another minute and I uncover the blasting cap. Fuck, I wish I could use my other hand. Even a little. My legs are screaming now, as if a thousand fire ants are crawling all over me. *You can do this.*

Four screws. Trembling fingers. Three. I drop the knife and almost set the whole damn thing off. Two. Inara's ragged breathing keeps me focused. One. And then...the cap falls into my palm.

"Inara." I hold up the detonator. "Help me. We...have to...get out of here."

She's at my side in a heartbeat, and though I know that steaming pile of shit could come back at any moment, I wrap my arm around her and bury my face against her neck long enough to drink in her scent. "Didn't think...we'd make it," I whisper.

"We're not out of this yet." She wedges her shoulder under my arm, and we stagger to our feet. My knees scream, and every time I breathe, my left shoulder sends stabbing pain into my back. As we wrench open the train car doors, a hail of bullets hits the metal.

Inara

We dive for the floor, Royce landing on his injured shoulder. The sickening pop as the bone slides back into its socket is muffled only by his tortured scream.

"Fuck!" We're trapped, Royce can barely move, and though he just diffused a fucking bomb to save our lives, there's still a very large brick of plastic explosive under the car and a crazy, dickless bastard outside. "I think he killed Ryker. I don't know about West. We have to get out of here."

"Go up," Royce says as he holds his shoulder and hisses out a breath. "There's...a hatch...in the ceiling."

"I'm not leaving you." After running away—was that only this morning?—and almost losing him, there's no way I'm going anywhere without him.

"I can't...keep up, baby. Can't climb. Can't run." With a grunt, Royce sits up, but the effort leaves him panting. "End this. You're the only one who can."

"Royce." Twining our fingers, I draw strength from the love in his eyes. "I was scared. And stupid. I never should have walked out on you. You're asking me to do it again."

"Not asking." He touches his forehead to mine. "He's unstable. Can't feel pain. Talked to himself a lot. Get him to make a mistake."

He's right. But that doesn't make it any easier for me to leave. Sliding my fingers through his hair, down to his neck, I steady him as I capture his bottom lip. My tongue explores, desperate, and he matches my need, his good arm banding around my back.

I can't let go, but Royce is strong enough for both of us, and with a final, agonizing groan, he pulls away as he presses the blasting cap into my hand. "Go."

A ladder runs the height of the car, and I climb the ten feet until I can hook my arms over one of the long beams traveling the ceiling. Swinging my legs up, I wrap my ankles around the thick metal, sliding until I'm suspended almost directly under the hatch.

My arms burn, but I manage to torque my body so I can flip the interior latch and shove the access panel open. Cool, night air wafts over my cheeks, and I spare Royce one final glance.

I love you.

I can't say the words. I want to...but...not like this. I pray I have the chance as I claw my way onto the train car's roof.

Pop, pop, pop. Three more shots. Not aimed at the rail car. *West is still alive.*

Crawling on my belly, I head for the edge of the roof. I need my earbud back. And my gun.

I hit the ground, tuck, and roll, the impact sailing up my legs. My first few steps are slow and awkward—part pain, part terror—and before I run out of cover, I pull the blasting cap from my pocket. Putting all I have into the throw, I send the tiny explosive sailing down the tracks a good sixty feet away from where I'm headed.

The *crack* and flash of light as it hits should give me just enough distraction. Muffled footfalls echo on metal far on my right, and I duck left, racing through the wide-open expanse.

Coop left all my shit right where I dropped it, and I scoop up the lot, then take off towards the Thunderbird. My sniper rifle's inside, and right now, that feels like my only chance.

Shoving the gritty earbud in my ear, I hiss, "West. Please tell me you're still alive."

"Can't get a shot. Fucker knows how to stay hidden. Fifty yards behind him. Don't know about Ryker." He punctuates his words with two quick shots, but the metal cars all around me distort the sound.

"If Coop's killed Ryker, I'm going to shoot him in the nuts before I end him," I mutter.

"Get in line."

At an all-out run, I slip through the gate. Skidding on the

rain-slicked pavement, slamming into the side of the car, I pray I'm fast enough. Except my rifle's not there. Pawing through my go-bag, I find my .44 Magnum. Not ideal, but better than this 9mm for distance.

"Coming to you. Stay alive."

Two of the longest minutes of my life later, I brace my back against a stack of shipping containers and risk a glance around the corner. Across the well-lit space, I spot West crouching against another rail car. "Where is he?" I ask.

West pops up, aims a shot towards a guard tower a hundred yards away, and Coop returns fire a second later. "Bad angle. Unless he stands up, I don't have a shot."

"He's unstable. Can't feel pain. Talked to himself a lot. Get him to make a mistake."

"I'll get him out in the open. Do me a favor. Don't miss." Gritting my teeth, I shove my emotions and fear into a tiny box I can lock and hide away. If I'm going to take a bullet, I need to believe Coop won't walk out of here alive. I meet West's gaze across the yard, and his eyes widen as he realizes what I'm going to do.

"Coop! Hey, shit-stain. You want me? Come get me." Pushing to my feet, I take two steps out into the open with my hands up. The .44 points to the sky, my finger clearly off the trigger.

Asphalt chips fly up, one slicing my cheek, another ripping through my pants and digging into my thigh as Coop's shot lands just in front of me. "You expect me to trust you, bitch?"

"No. I expect you to kill me. That's what you want, isn't it? All I care about is Royce." A shadow from the top of Coop's head falls over the guard tower railing. Just a little farther. "You're right. I left you. West and Ryker mean more to me than you ever did. Oh, and our new guy? He's twenty-five. A baby. But he's more of a man than you'll ever be."

Coop stands, a long-range rifle pointed directly at my head. *Please, West. Don't let me die.*

"I don't have a fucking shot."

The words turn my blood to ice. In my periphery, West leaps up from his hiding spot and rounds the corner.

"Goodbye, Inara," Coop shouts.

Royce. I love you.

I look death in the eyes. The sound of the shot reverberates all around me, and I brace for the pain. But as if in slow motion, Coop folds forward over the railing, the rifle clattering as it tumbles down the tower, catching on a strut fifteen feet off the ground.

West reaches my side, and we both stare at the lone figure on top of a rail car with a perfect line of sight to Coop's body.

"Don't just stand there," Ryker shouts. "Make sure he's good and dead, then let's get Royce and get the fuck out of here."

Royce holds a two-foot long piece of metal like a baseball bat as I yank the door open, but it clatters to the floor when I call his name. "It's over," I manage. "He's dead."

Helping the man I love out of the car, we both stumble, and I almost collapse under his weight, but Ryker's at my side a heartbeat later, steadying us. "Give me your phone," he says. "Then take the car and get Royce back to his place. West and I will clean this shit up. In an hour, expect a house call from a Dr. Reynolds. This whole thing here?" He gestures around us. "It never happened."

I nod and hand the phone over. "You know how to reach me."

Ryker limps away, pain obvious in the set of his shoulders, and I brace Royce against the side of the car. "Give me a minute?"

"Go."

As I catch Ryker, he glares at me. "You disobeying orders?"

"Thank you." I don't care that he'll pull away. I don't care that

I might never hear the end of this. Throwing my arms around him, I wait for the protest, but after he draws in a sharp breath, he returns the embrace. "I owe you my life. And Royce's."

"We're even now." His words are thick with emotion, almost a whisper, and after a quick squeeze, he turns and heads for the tower.

21

Inara

I PACE and fidget as the doctor examines Royce. He fell asleep—
or passed out—as soon as I got him to the car. Once we got to his
place, he woke up, and managed to stay awake through a hot
shower and me maneuvering him into bed, but he's had half a
dozen seizures since. We've barely spoken, and watching his face
contort in pain as Dr. Reynolds checks his range of motion is too
much for me.

Stalking out to the kitchen, I pull down a bottle of scotch and
two glasses. I haven't eaten all day, and this is probably a terrible
idea, but I'm about to come out of my skin. The liquor burns a
path down my throat, and I brace my arms against the counter,
bending over as a wave of dizziness threatens.

"Whoa there," Dr. Reynolds says as he takes my arm. "I
thought I only had one patient tonight."

"Royce?" Shaking him off, I take two quick steps back, sliding
on the tile as the pajama pants I stole from Royce's dresser are at
least four inches too long for me. The cut on my cheek is the

worst of my injuries, and a couple of butterfly bandages took care of it.

The doctor's gentle smile loosens the vise tightened around my heart. "He needs rest. Can't say I'd *advise* the scotch from a medical standpoint, but you both look like you need it. I want to get an MRI of that shoulder in a few days to be sure, but if there's any lasting damage, it won't be severe. He was lucky."

Schooling my features lest I break down into a blubbering mess in the middle of the kitchen, I offer the doctor my hand. "Thank you. Ryker—"

"He and I go way back." With a chuckle, he shakes his head when I start to speak again. "And that's all I'll ever say about him. Royce has my card. If anything changes—if the seizures don't stop by tomorrow, if his pain is too severe, if the swelling is worse in the morning—you call me."

I manage a nod, walk him to the door, and secure the deadbolt. Sinking down against the wall, I allow myself to crumble, huge, body-wracking sobs escaping silently as tears stream down my cheeks.

And then, Royce is next to me, sitting on the floor, pulling me against his bare chest. Careful not to brush the sling holding his shoulder immobile, I wrap my arms around his waist and curl into him.

"I'm okay, baby. Promise." His words are still a little slow, a little slurred, but when I tip my head to meet his gaze, his eyes are clear. And full of love. "Kind of cold down here, though. Bed's warm. Got something...need to ask you."

I prop pillows against his headboard, then press myself as close as I can to his good side. The words I long to say won't come. Every time I try, the lump in my throat chokes me.

Royce runs the backs of his fingers along my cheek, then down my arm. "You look better in that t-shirt than I ever did."

The laugh that bubbles up surprises me, and I press a kiss to his chapped lips. "It's the only thing I have besides tactical gear. I hope you don't want it back anytime soon."

"It's yours." He closes his eyes with a sigh.

I draw in a sharp breath. My heart is his. If I don't tell him soon...it's just going to get harder. Cupping his cheek, his stubble rough against my palm, I whisper, "Royce. Stay with me for just a minute."

"Not going anywhere, baby." His blue eyes lock on mine, the gray streaks so bright they're almost platinum, and he smiles. "Don't want you to either. Move in."

"What?" I expected him to ask about Ryker. Why we couldn't call the cops. Who killed Coop. Not... "move in."

"Move in. I know...it's soon. But if you sign...a year lease...I don't want to wait...that long. You're it for me, baby."

Careful not to jostle his shoulder, I straddle him, and even after everything he's been through today, he hardens, sending a flood of warmth to my core.

"I love you, Royce." My voice cracks, but once the words escape, the heavy weight on my chest disappears. "I should have told you last night. Should have shown you one more painting... the one I only realized when I'd finished...was us. You're my heart. My strength. You understand me—even when I don't understand myself."

"Is that a yes?" His brows arch, though there's a hint of fear behind his gaze. Shit.

Leaning close, my hands braced on either side of him, I brush my lips to his ear. "I'm pretty stubborn, soldier. You couldn't get me to leave if you tried."

As he fists my hair and claims my mouth with a searing kiss, a piece of me I never knew was missing falls into place.

"I love you," I whisper. "This is where I belong."

Royce sleeps easily as I lean against the door jamb with a cup of coffee. I could watch him all day, but as much as I love this t-shirt, I need clothes. Moisturizer. Deodorant.

Padding out to the kitchen for a refill, I boot up Hidden Agenda's laptop. Time to do some online shopping. Five hundred dollars later—why is makeup so damn expensive?—I'm contemplating pizza delivery when there's a soft knock at the door.

My heart races as I check the peephole. Ryker has a duffel bag slung over his shoulder, black glasses hiding his eyes.

Without a word, I invite him in.

"Brought you some clothes," he says as he sets the bag down next to the couch. "Your phone's in there too. Along with some stuff for Royce."

"Th-thanks. Can I...get you some coffee?" I don't know how to react. Ryker's said more to me in the past twenty-four hours than he has in the past year.

"Sure." He shoves his hands into his pockets, skirting the couch to stare out at Lake Washington.

Mug in hand, I approach warily. "You okay, Ry?"

"I'll live." After a sip, he gives me the once over. "You look like shit."

"Well, I lost my home and all my stuff, and Royce almost died because I fucked up in Colombia—"

"You didn't fuck up." Sinking down onto the couch, he rubs a hand over his bald head. "I did."

"What?" Ryker's bulk fills half the couch, and I wedge myself into the corner and tuck my legs under me. "I'm the one who hesitated."

"I should have fired his ass a year ago. He came to me after Landow died, demanding I put him on infiltration instead of comms. When I said no, he threw one of the laptops across the room, told me to go fuck myself, and then got himself arrested on his drive home for going ninety on I-5, then screaming at the police officer who stopped him."

Shock steals any response, and Ryker stares into his mug. "He went off book in Colombia because he thought he knew better than West. Than me. He blamed you because...you were the last person he saw. Maybe you hesitated. Maybe not. I've replayed that day about a thousand times in the past twenty-four hours. The timing of the shots." He taps his temple as his eyes unfocus. "In Hell, I trained myself to remember almost anything I heard. The last book I read before I was captured? *Memory Mastery.* That's how I escaped. Memorized every guard's footsteps, the pattern of the doors slamming shut as each of the assholes walked through the tunnels, the way voices changed based on who was in charge for the day."

"Shit, Ry. That's... Wow."

"Bottom line. Coop was a loose cannon before he was captured. After he escaped?" He shakes his head. "West and I found his hole. Fucknut was sleeping—and pissing—in one of the old shipping containers. Living off jerky and protein bars. Had a dozen notebooks filled with plans for each of us. Including Cam." With a snort, the corner of Ryker's mouth turns up slightly. "I've never seen West lose his shit before."

We finish our coffee, and I glance down the hallway. "What happened to you last night? Coop said you were down."

Ryker pushes to his feet and stifles a wince. Pulling up his tight black t-shirt, he reveals a thick bandage under his left arm. "Pissant shot me, and I fell off a tanker car. Pretty sure I passed out for a couple of minutes. Dude doesn't know what dead looks like."

"You didn't respond on comms."

"Lost my earbud when I hit the ground," he says with a scowl as he tugs his shirt back into place.

"There more of that coffee?" Royce asks as he limps into the room.

Ryker heads for the door as I wrap my arms around Royce's waist. "I'm ordering pizza, Ry. Want to stay?"

"No. I need to take the van to my detailer. It's...a little bloody. I'll be in touch, Inara." He offers Royce his hand. "I don't think we ever formally met."

"Thank you," Royce says as the two men shake. "I...don't know what went down after Inara left the rail car, but I vaguely remember something about you and West cleaning the whole mess up. A lot of last night's sort of fuzzy."

Ryker looks uncomfortable, but nods. "Getting the cops involved...they'd shut down Hidden Agenda without a second thought. We took care of it. That headstone Coop's family paid for? Well, now it stands over his body."

Silence stretches until Ryker's phone buzzes. With a quick glance at the screen, he sighs. "Gotta go. No training until further notice. I think we all need a little time. Couple weeks, at least. Maybe longer."

Though I don't want to leave his side, I unwind my arms from Royce's waist and follow Ryker to the door. "Ry?"

"Yeah?" The look on his face—I've never seen such sorrow in his eyes—shocks me.

"Don't go dark on us. Okay?" I don't know why I ask, but something's wrong. Something sending him into an abyss I worry will swallow him whole.

Four days later

My new key slides into the front door, and when I step inside, the scents of spicy tomato sauce and garlic bread greet me. "Royce?"

He ducks his head out of the kitchen with a smile. "Welcome home. I hope you're hungry."

"I could get used to this." Dropping my bag next to the couch, I shrug out of my coat. "But you're supposed to be taking it easy."

"Soft tissue damage only. Doc cleared me to—" he slides an arm around my waist and tugs me against him, "—resume all normal activities."

"*All* normal activities?" I'm starved, but not for food. These past few days, we've watched a dozen movies on Netflix, ordered takeout from every restaurant in the neighborhood, and tried to forget how close we both came to dying.

Though we've had some stellar—and R-rated—make-out sessions, we've yet to make love, and I don't know if I can take another night where I wake with his name on my lips and my clit aching.

Carefully, he slides his left hand into my hair. "All of them." His fingers tighten, and the pinpricks of pain send desire flooding the lace between my thighs. Thank God for overnight shipping and a damn good insurance company.

Walking me backwards down the hall, he holds my gaze, and the silver flecks in his eyes darken. "I need you, Inara. And dinner won't be ready for an hour."

"There's a lot we can do in an hour." Flicking open the button on his Levi's, I grin, and when the backs of my legs hit the bed, I lean into his kiss.

Firm lips claim me, and I yield to the light dance of his tongue. As I shove his pants down his hips, he groans, and his erection presses against my thigh.

"I want you naked," he roughs out and tugs the teal sweater over my head. "Oh, fuck." The red lace bra can't hide my peaked nipples, and he rolls one between his fingers, drawing a long, low moan from my throat. "You and lace. I'll never get enough."

"There's more." Dropping my gaze for just a moment, I quirk a brow. "I was going to have you tonight even if I had to tie you down so you couldn't move."

Royce takes a step back, and I kick off my shoes and step out of my pants. When I look up, shock stills my movements. He's holding a pair of padded cuffs almost identical to the ones that burned in the fire—still attached to my headboard, if I recall. "You're not the only one who can work a little online shopping magic," he says with a wink. A quick twist of his fingers behind my back and the bra falls away. "These are for later, though. First, I'm going to taste you."

Guiding me down to the bed, he worships my breasts, lavishing attention on each nipple until I'm begging, and my arousal slicks my thighs. "Hands braced behind you. I want you to see everything I do to you."

From this position, leaning back with my ass half off the bed and my legs spread wide, he gets his wish, and the sight of his tongue teasing the edge of my thong, his kisses trailing slowly along the top of my thigh until he slides the soaked lace off my hips and thrusts two fingers deep inside me is the sexiest thing I've ever seen.

"Come for me, baby." With a swipe of his tongue, I implode, and I see only him as endless waves of pleasure threaten to drown me.

An hour later, I carry two plates of lasagna and garlic bread to the table, wearing only one of his army t-shirts and a stupid smile I can't seem to wipe away.

He managed a pair of jeans, and his bare chest gives me all sorts of ideas that don't involve food, but we're going to need our strength for the rest of the night, so I sink down onto the chair across from him and admire the cut of his muscles as he pours me a glass of wine.

In my memories, he struggles to breathe as Coop laughs, and I shudder, my chest tight.

"Inara?" Royce reaches for my hand, and as if he can sense my thoughts, he holds on tight. "Breathe, baby. We survived."

We did. And today, I saw my shrink. Royce didn't know about the appointment, but tonight, when we're lying in bed, our legs intertwined, I'll tell him everything. Including the peace I've made with who I am. I can't shove all my emotions inside the little box they used to fit into. I'll never be able to do that again. But the work I do with Hidden Agenda...the team—the family— I've found myself a part of...they don't need me to be a statue anymore. They need the woman I am now. The one who knows emotions don't make you weak. They make you stronger.

With a gentle tug, he pulls me into his lap, and I run my fingers through his hair, over the scar behind his ear, and down to his neck. Dipping my head, I brush my lips to his.

"I love you, Royce. With you...I'm who I'm supposed to be."

Hi,

Thank you for reading *In Her Sights*. Inara and Royce are safe, and soon, they're going to be attending Cam and West's wedding.

But Ryker...he's headed for a world of hurt. You never really escape Hell. When he finds a ghost from his past in trouble, he'll risk everything—including his sanity—to save her.

Sign up for my Unstoppable Newsletter on my website to be

the first to know when Ryker's book comes out! Oh, and you'll also get West and Cam's wedding bonus scene as soon as I release it!

Love,
Patricia

ACKNOWLEDGMENTS

I'd like to give a shoutout to my Unstoppable Forces Team. These super fans kept me motivated, and during that long, last night of writing, a few of them gave me some very inventive curses for Inara, Royce, and Ryker to use.

Kayce contributed dickless bastard and fuckwad.

Elizabeth offered up fuckstick.

Vickie contributed steaming pile of shit.

Michele offered up shitstain.

Thanks, Unstoppable Forces! You rock!
Love,
Patricia

ALSO BY PATRICIA D. EDDY

By the Fates

Check out the By the Fates series if you love dark and steamy tales of witches, devils, and an epic battle between good and evil.

By the Fates, Freed

Destined, a By the Fates Story

By the Fates, Fought

By the Fates, Fulfilled

In Blood

If you love hot Italian vampires and and a human who can hold her own against beings far stronger, then the In Blood series is for you.

Secrets in Blood

Revelations in Blood — Coming in mid 2018

Elemental Shifter

Hot werewolves and strong, powerful elementals. What's not to love?

A Shift in the Water

A Shift in the Air

Contemporary and Erotic Romances

Holidays and Heroes

Beauty isn't only skin deep and not all scars heal. Come swoon over sexy vets and the men and women who love them.

Mistletoe and Mochas

Love and Libations

Away From Keyboard

Dive into a steamy mix of geekery and military might with the men and women of Emerald City Security and North-West Protective Services.

Breaking His Code

In Her Sights

Restrained

Do you like to be tied up? Or read about characters who do? Enjoy a fresh BDSM series that will leave you begging for more.

In His Silks

Christmas Silks

All Tied Up for New Year's

In His Collar

ABOUT ME

I've always made up stories. Sometimes I even acted them out. I probably shouldn't admit that my childhood best friend and I used to run around the backyard pretending to fly in our Invisible Jet and rescue Steve Trevor. Oops.

Now that I'm too old to spin around in circles with felt magic bracelets on my wrists, I put "pen to paper" instead. Figuratively, at least. Fingers to keyboard is more accurate.

Outside of my writing, I'm a professional editor, a software geek, a singer (in the shower only), a beginner guitar player, and a runner. I love red wine, scotch (neat, please), and cider. Seattle is my home, and I share an old house with three spoiled cats.

I'm on my fourth—fifth?—rewatching of the modern *Doctor Who*, and I think one particular quote from that show sums up my entire life.

"We're all stories, in the end. Make it a good one, eh?" — *The Eleventh Doctor, Doctor Who*

I hope your story is brilliant.

You can reach me all over the web...
patriciadeddy.com
patricia@patriciadeddy.com

facebook.com/patriciadeddyauthor

twitter.com/patriciadeddy

instagram.com/patriciadeddy

bookbub.com/profile/patricia-d-eddy

amazon.com/author/pdeddy